# Doodles Lanhorn

## and the Search for the Missing Artifact

RUSSELL D. BERNSTEIN

ISBN: 978-1-938998-85-0 (paperback)
ISBN: 978-1-938998-90-4 (hardcover)

Library of Congress Control Number: 2016952846

Published by:
Hannacroix Creek Books, Inc.
1127 High Ridge Road, #110
Stamford, Connecticut 06905 USA
http://www.hannacroixcreekbooks.com
hannacroix@aol.com

Follow us on twitter:
http://www.twitter.com/hannacroixcreek

*Dedication*

To my beautiful and supportive wife Holly, and to my wonderful daughters Brianne and Sydney. You are my everything. I tip my Wizartry hat to you.

# CHAPTER 1

D oodles Lanhorn ran through the halls of Lincoln Middle School, holding his backpack with one hand, because of the broken strap, and juggling his textbooks in the other. He was late again. Mr. Bloom would not be happy. As he ran, Doodles' long red hair kept falling over his eyes, obstructing his view.

He quickened his pace, skidding around a hallway corner, and nearly flying into a wall of lockers. A few books fell to the floor and he hastily picked them up, continuing on through the corridor. The janitor must have recently mopped the floor because it was very slippery, Doodles thought. Just what he needed: more challenges. Even though it was still early in the school year, he already had the feeling that last year would seem like nothing compared to this year in the eighth grade. Teachers were stricter, time management was tougher, and the kids were struggling once again, now that they were the older kids, to find which group they fit into.

One would think that since he had saved Inner Earth twice, was only one test away from becoming a fully-fledged member of the Wizarts, and was well on his way to becoming one of the most talented Wizarts ever, he would be confident and capable enough to handle the last year of middle school. Unfortunately, this was not the case. Doodles felt even more out of place and awkward this year than he had in previous grades. Many of his classmates had changed a lot over the summer. Some of the boys had started to grow significantly taller, while many of the girls didn't look like little girls any more. But Doodles pretty much looked the same. At least he thought so.

Luckily for Doodles and his best friends, Darren and Laura, Brandon, the class bully, had been sent off to military school to straighten out his behavioral issues. Brandon would have to repeat last year and get very good grades before they would allow him to go on to the next grade.

The week before school started, Laura and Darren had talked about a fresh start for their last year of middle school. They shared their excitement and fears, trying to mentally prepare for what they had heard being a senior was like. They thought they were pretty well prepared, but no amount of talking could have prepared them for the actual experience.

"Get out of the way!" one of the seniors said, throwing an elbow into Doodles' gut as he passed, knocking the air out of Doodles' lungs. Some things never seemed to change, Doodles thought. He was tempted to use his Wizartry powers to create something to use to get back at the kid, but he restrained himself at the last second. He couldn't break the rules. If people found out about Wizartry, Doodles knew there could be grave consequences.

As Doodles took a sip of water from the hall water fountain, trying to cool down before he continued to home room, he heard his name being called.

"Mr. Lanhorn!" It was the school principal, Mr. Irving. He had to be in his seventies by now. It was amazing that the man still wanted to work in this environment with surly teenagers and all of their drama and nonsense when clearly he could have retired a while back. Hollyport's Lincoln Middle School was not exactly one of the state's top rated institutions.

Mr. Irving made a show of shooing the kids off to their classrooms and then walked slowly toward Doodles, his back slightly hunched from years of poor posture. His wispy, long grey hair bounced as he walked, his ashen, grey eyes narrow and intense. His finely-polished shoes squeaked on the hallway floor. Doodles imagined he was about to be lectured to on being tardy to class.

"Mr. Lanhorn. Someone is here to see you," the Principal said in a gruff voice. He gave a quick smile and without waiting, he turned around and headed back to his office, mumbling something about the hallways always being dirty.

Doodles hesitated and then followed. Were his parents here? Was something wrong? He looked around but he was alone in the hallway now. The rest of the stragglers had gone into their classrooms. At least he wouldn't be harassed in the hallways now that it was empty, Doodles thought.

He took his time getting to the Principal's office, trying to guess who would be visiting him during school hours but it was pointless to speculate. Better to just get this over with.

He walked into the open doorway and stopped. His heart suddenly pounded in his chest. There, sitting on one of the chairs, was the Mayor of Hollyport! He had a smug expression on his face. His meaty hands were clasped calmly on his lap. He was dressed in a black suit and yellow tie. He had the same jocular appearance he always wore making people think he was a warm and friendly man who loved Hollyport and the people who lived there. But, after everything that had happened over the summer, Doodles knew better.

Doodles wanted to yell out, to tell the Principal how terrible a person the Mayor was. The Mayor must have sensed Doodles' uneasiness because his smile widened into a smirk that gave Doodles the creeps. The Mayor knew he had him. Since the Wizarts had erased the memory of everyone who had been led into Inner Earth, no one would believe all of the despicable things the Mayor had done trying to take over the magical world that most Wizarts inhabited. Telling on the Mayor would also mean revealing Wizartry and Inner Earth again, and Doodles couldn't do that. Unfortunately, the Mayor, Rita, and Alanso had all gotten away before they could be captured so their memory of the events had not been erased.

"What do you want?" Doodles asked.

Mr. Irving's eyes narrowed. "Now, Mr. Lanhorn," he said. "That is no way to greet a visitor, especially one so esteemed as our Mayor."

"But he is..." Doodles began to protest and had to restrain himself against all of his instincts.

"That's quite all right," the Mayor said. "He must be star struck meeting a mayor. That's all."

The Mayor stood up and held out a hand for Doodles to shake. "Please, call me Shane."

Thinking about calling the Mayor "Shane" was just too weird, and if he did it around the other kids, they might mistakenly think Doodles and the Mayor were friends. Doodles didn't want to be associated with the Mayor at all. The best he could do would be to call him Mr. Derringer.    "Doodles?" Mr. Irving said. The Mayor was still holding out his hand.

Doodles hesitated. He couldn't come up with an excuse to get out of shaking the Mayor's hand without seeming rude. In that moment, Doodles remembered everything that the Mayor had put him through: kidnapping his family, betraying all of Wizartry's secrets, bribing police officers, and giving everyone access to Inner Earth. The man was a horrible person and a corrupt and selfish thug.

With no other choice, Doodles bit his tongue and shook the Mayor's hand.

"Mayor Derringer tells me he is switching from politics to... Well, I'll just let you tell him," Mr. Irving said, looking to the Mayor.

Mayor Derringer gave a smile and shrugged. "Been thinking about it for some time. Mr. Irving and I have been good friends for years now. In fact, he was an integral part of my campaign a few years back."

"I hardly think I was the main reason you won," Mr. Irving said. "Just doing my share to help a friend."

"You're being too modest," the Mayor said.

Doodles couldn't believe what was going on. If only his father were here. He would know what to do. Even Laura, his best friend, would come up with something to say.

"What are you getting at?" Doodles asked.

"Ah, you are to the point," the Mayor said. "I like that. When the Board of Education became aware of my decision not to run for mayor again, and of Mr. Irving's wish to retire, they made me a very generous offer. So generous an offer that I could hardly refuse. I am going to be taking over as your school principal, Doodles." The Mayor let that information sink in, watching gleefully as Doodles squirmed with discomfort.

"I am going to be making some changes here," Mayor Derringer continued. "One of those changes has to do with you, Doodles."

Doodles didn't like where this was heading. Every time the Mayor mentioned his name, his skin crawled with a sickening feeling. The man was a criminal. Whatever he was planning would not be good.

"I hear you are quite the artist," the Mayor said, clearly playing dumb. "I want to start a special art class for gifted students like you."

Now Doodles knew he was definitely up to something, but there was nothing that Doodles could call him out on, yet.

"Exciting stuff, isn't it?" Mr. Irving asked.

Doodles pinched himself to make sure this wasn't some twisted nightmare he was having. Nope, that hurt. This was all too real.

# CHAPTER 2

"You're kidding, right?" Laura asked. She was reading a book on Native American history, a thick, red, leather-bound hardcover. She dropped it on the floor of her living room when Doodles told her what had happened at school.

"I wish I was," Doodles replied. He started to bite his finger-nails nervously.

"It doesn't make any sense," Laura yelled out.

"Is everything okay?" Laura's mother called from the next room.

"Yes!" Laura called back. She lowered her voice. "We have to tell someone."

"Who do we tell? Who would believe us?" Doodles asked. "Besides, if we tell, we risk Wizartry being discovered again, and that can't happen."

"Well, we have to do something!" Laura exclaimed. "We can't just let him get away with whatever it is he's planning!"

"I know that," Doodles replied. "But he hasn't done anything yet. We'll just have to wait for him to slip up and do something awful. Then we will bring the hard evidence to the school board, the police, or newspapers of the Wizarts, to somebody."

"I don't like this one bit," Laura said. "Does Darren know yet?" Doodles shook his head.

"He is going to flip out when we tell him," she said.

"Yeah, I'm not looking forward to that," Doodles admitted.

"What about your parents?" Laura asked.

"I already told them. They are angry but they said not to do anything until they discuss options with the Wizartry Council. It's too early to make a move on him now," Doodles explained. Doodles knew that, although his parents weren't Wizarts themselves, their advice and connections with the Wizartry world gave them the opportunity to provide valuable advice.

Laura paced around a few times and then turned sharply to Doodles saying, "I just don't get it. Why would he risk showing his face around here again?"

Doodles knew when Laura was getting upset. She did this thing with her face where her nose would crinkle up and her eyes narrowed. Doodles found it cute, but he would never admit that to her.

"He's here because he wants something. I know he is. I can almost feel it in my bones. The man is greedy and selfish," Doodles said. "Trust me. I don't like this any more than you do, but we have to be patient. If we lose our cool, things could go badly."

Doodles thought back to all the times he had acted too rashly without thinking things through. He wasn't sure whether or not this newfound sense of patience was from him maturing or from his prior experiences. Either way, as hard as it was to be patient at a time like this, it was the right way to handle the situation.

"Do you think Alanso and Rita are with him?" Laura asked.

"I doubt it," Doodles replied. "They were only using him, and the Wizartry Council is scouring Inner Earth and Hollyport for any sign of them."

"Are you going to let him put you in that art class?" Laura asked, finally standing still.

"What choice do I have?" Doodles asked. "Look, as soon as he slips up, we'll get him."

"I don't like this one bit, Doodles Lanhorn," Laura said, hands on her hips. "He is dangerous and I'm afraid he might be looking for a way to punish you for ruining his plans to take over Inner Earth before."

"What do you suggest?" Doodles asked.

She paced around a few more times, picking up some books off the floor and placing them back on the bookshelf. Doodles always thought it was funny that she paced and cleaned while concentrating. He couldn't count the number of times she had accidently straightened up his room while they were planning something. She always had that certain look in her eyes when she was deep in thought. Her eyes had an intense stare, her brow furrowed in concentration. After a minute or so of pacing, she stopped abruptly. "I have an idea," she said. "We'll have to get Darren up to speed on the plan, too."

Doodles smiled. He could always count on his friends to come up with plans.

"We can spy on him with the help of Wizartry. He is overly confident. If we can catch him on camera saying or doing something strange, we've got him!" she said.

Doodles began to move his hands. They moved in fluid motions, traces of light appearing. The air shimmered, there was a popping sound, and a beautiful bouquet of flowers appeared in his hand. Doodles had mastered Wizartry with just the use of his hands while other Wizarts required a special paint and brush for their creations to come to life. "This is for being the best friend ever," Doodles said, holding the extraordinarily colorful flowers out to her.

"Show off," she said. But she was smiling.

# CHAPTER 3

D oodles sat in the back row of the classroom. It was one of the oldest wings of the school and the furniture was outdated and in dire need of repair or replacement. The chair he was sitting on threatened to come apart at the legs. He noticed a student who had used this desk in years past had carved quite a few not so nice comments into the surface of the wood, leaving deep grooves.

He was one of ten students in the class. All of them were eighth graders, like Doodles, sitting there just as confused as he was. None of them had signed up for this class but there it was on their schedules. The teacher hadn't arrived yet, and most of the students sat there noisily talking and joking about what they might be doing there and who their teacher would be. Doodles reckoned they were trying to judge how much they could get away with.

Someone had scribbled the words, "Art Class" on the chalkboard, a rather vague description, Doodles thought. Doodles checked his backpack to make sure Laura's camera was in there. The bag was positioned so that he could record the front of the classroom through the bag's opening. Hopefully the teacher wouldn't notice. He and Laura had discussed recording everything, getting as much evidence as possible, having the camera at school at all times in case Mr. Derringer slipped up which was all vital to the plan. Doodles shivered a little bit.

On top of worrying about the Mayor, Doodles' elderly Wizart mentor, Riddley, had informed Doodles that he would soon be given his third and final test to become a Wizart. Talk about stress. Aunt Martha and Uncle Roger had warned him that eighth grade was a lot of pressure, but no one knew how much pressure it was to deal with eighth grade and Wizartry at the same time.

Someone hit Doodles in the back of the head with a spitball. He tried to ignore it, focusing instead on a text book. A few seconds later something hard hit him on the side of the head. It was impossible to ignore. He yelled out in shock and looked down. Someone had thrown their shoe at him. Doodles rubbed at his head as a kid got up and retrieved the shoe.

"Whoops," the kid said sarcastically. The rest of the kids snickered. Doodles hoped the teacher would come in soon before things got worse.

"Enough, guys," a girl right behind Doodles said loudly. The other kids laughed and then went back to talk among themselves.

"Hi, I'm Samantha," the kid said, holding out her hand. Doodles shook it in surprise. No one except Laura or Darren had ever stood up for him.

"Doodles," Doodles replied. For some reason he didn't understand felt his face getting red and his heart beating faster. He had to try to keep his mouth closed and to avoid sounding like a complete dolt. Samantha was breathtakingly beautiful. She was almost as tall as Doodles, with dark, jet-black hair that fell to her shoulders and sat neatly there as if done perfectly. She had an angular face and warm, inviting eyes. Those mesmerizing black eyes were almost as beautiful as her tanned skin.

"I know who you are," Samantha said. "Just try to keep out of trouble. I'll keep them off your back."

"Thanks," Doodles said. She actually knew who he was! Hopefully that didn't mean she heard all the terrible rumors kids started about him. Doodles didn't know what to say next so he turned around and pretended to read his textbook again. He wasn't used to random kindness, especially from someone so pretty.

Thankfully the door opened and the students looked up. A woman walked in. She wasn't anyone Doodles recognized from last year's faculty. She walked with her head held high and a friendly smile on her face. She was slim and tall, probably in her mid-thirties, Doodles wagered. She was rather pretty with dark hair like Laura.

She smiled at the students and placed a few books and a bag on top of the teacher's desk.

"Please, quiet down everyone!" she said.

The other students slowly quieted down and settled into their seats.

"Hello, Class," she said in a soft and pleasant voice. The other students murmured "Hello" and Doodles joined in. Doodles was feeling anxious. He felt the need to distrust her, but she was making it hard to do so. If the Mayor had anything to do with hiring her then she couldn't be a good person, but she seemed genuinely kind.

"I am Mrs. Roberts. I will be your art teacher. This class is a new initiative, a pilot class courtesy of your new Principal," she explained. "You have been hand-selected to be a part of this class and I am sure you will all make your parents proud."

Doodles couldn't help feeling that her eyes lingered on him longer than any other student when she talked. Was he just being paranoid?

"We are going to make art come alive in this class," Mrs. Roberts continued. Doodles was sure now that she was looking right at him. He gulped.

* * *

Laura, Darren, and Doodles sat at one of the outside picnic tables during lunch. Darren nervously gobbled up his spaghetti and meatballs, slurping annoyingly loud. Doodles picked at his lunch, while Laura hadn't even opened hers.

"You're sure she was staring right at you?" Laura asked Doodles.

Doodles nodded. "We could check the recording later but I'm positive," he replied.

Darren finally put his fork down and said, "I almost wish you guys didn't tell me what is going on. I'm having enough trouble fitting in here as it is."

Laura gave him a pat on the back. "We'll figure this out, buddy. Together, like we always do."

Doodles gave a look around to make sure no one was nearby. They had selected one of the picnic tables at the back side of the patio area located just outside the cafeteria's side door. Not many people sat all the way over here.

"We should do some investigating after school today," Doodles whispered.

Laura nodded. Darren hesitated and then nodded too.

"We can do this. We just have to be careful about it," Darren said.

"I'm not sure where we should start looking," Doodles said.

"We can try to check out Mr. Derringer's office. He is just starting to get settled in. Maybe he will be careless and leave something incriminating," Laura said.

Darren shook his head. "His office will be locked," he said. "We'll have to find a way in. Maybe the window?"

Laura laughed. "With Doodles' Wizartry skills, we won't need to open the lock or crawl through a window."

"Hey guys," a voice suddenly sounded behind them.

They all turned around in surprise.

"It's okay. This is Samantha. She's new this year. She's awesome," Doodles explained to his friends, his face going just a little red again. He realized that that was probably not the right thing to say.

Samantha laughed and sat down. "I don't know about awesome, but I try." She shrugged innocently. Samantha had a smile that instantly made Doodles feel happy.

Laura gave Samantha a suspicious look as Samantha turned and looked into Doodles' eyes.

"What are you all talking about?" Samantha asked.

Doodles began, "We are going on a mission to..."

Laura shouted, "Doodles! What are you doing? You know we can't share our plans with anyone!"

"We can trust her," Doodles explained. "She stood up for me in class."

"Doesn't mean she won't tell on us," Laura said, crossing her arms. "You barely know her."

Samantha smiled at her and winked. "Doodles is my new friend, and any friends of his are my friends, too. You can trust me."

"Yeah, guys, see?" Doodles asked. He wanted to impress her, to tell her everything he had accomplished and knew. "We need all the help we can get."

Laura gave Samantha a dirty look. Samantha smiled even brighter.

"The suspense is killing me," Samantha finally said. "What is it?"

Doodles took a deep breath. "This will take a lot of explaining to catch you up, Samantha."

He was nervous, but this time he had not only his best friends with him from the start, but also a new friend. As he had learned before, together he and his friends could accomplish anything when they put their minds to it.

# CHAPTER 4

The four kids waited for the students to clear the school. The Principal's office door was locked. Everyone had gone home. They had to hide in a janitor closet to make sure no one knew they were still there.

"I think it's clear," Darren whispered.

"Yep, sure looks like it," Samantha said.

Doodles peeked through the crack. "Hold on," Doodles said. Sure enough, a janitor walked down the hallway, sweeping a mop back and forth in a lazy fashion. The janitor approached the closet. "We have to hide!" Doodles said in a frantic whisper.

Laura looked around. There were only a handful of cleaning supplies. "There's nowhere to hide. Do something, Doodles!"

The janitor was getting closer now. He was humming a song in a low murmur. Doodles began to move his hands, swirling lights following his every move. Samantha watched him with wide, curious eyes.

"Hurry, Doodles! He's almost here!" Darren whispered. "Do you want me to run for it? I could distract him and you guys can get away."

"No," Doodles said, his face set in determination. "I'm almost done." He tried to look confident for Samantha.

Doodles finished his last hand movement and there was a popping sound. The air shimmered and a wall appeared, the exact same off-white color as the rest of the walls in the closet.

Doodles had left just enough space for them to squeeze through.

"Don't make a sound," Doodles whispered.

The janitor closet opened and the janitor stepped in. He looked around, whistled a few times, and then threw the mop and bucket into the corner and closed the door. Doodles realized he had been holding his breath and let it out.

"That was close," Darren said. He peeked out through the crack again. "Coast is clear."

"So cool!" Samantha exclaimed. "Wizartry is amazing!" She wrapped her arms around Doodles and gave him a big squeeze. "We are going to be best friends, Doodles!"

Doodles blushed and Laura rolled her eyes.

They waited another few moments just to make sure and then crept out of the janitor closet. The four of them made their way down the rest of the hallway and stood in front of the Principal's office door. "Okay, let me just make sure I have some dissolving ink on me to erase the door I draw."

Doodles rummaged through his pockets and pulled out a clear vial of blue liquid. "Got it. All set," he said.

He then painted a door and opened it. When they were all inside, he poured half the vial of dissolving ink to make his creation disappear in case someone came by. They would need the remaining half when he drew a door to get out.

They stood in the Principal's office. It was unnervingly quiet. The dark blue carpet that their new Principal had installed was lush and absorbed the sound of their footsteps. A long desk in the corner was made of finely carved wood and kept immaculately clean and shiny. Doodles scoffed at the fact that Mr. Derringer had spent a lot of the school's budget money to make his office more elegant than any other school principal had ever done. It wasn't really a surprise seeing as his last visit to the Mayor's house showed that it was full of expensive art, elaborate sculptures and statues.

There were a few piles of papers and books on the corner of the desk, neatly stacked. Laura pointed to them and she and Doodles began to go through them. Darren looked through a large file cabinet on the other side of the room. Samantha stood near the door, listening for anyone that might be heading to the office.

"Put everything back the way you found it," Doodles warned. "We can't let him know someone was in here."

"Wait a second!" Laura exclaimed. "Isn't that your book?" She grabbed a book out from under one of the piles of papers and folders that were on the desk and held it up. It was the book filled with beautiful illustrations from master Wizarts, the book that had been given to him on his last birthday by his uncle and aunt. This was the book that had led Doodles on his first adventure into the fascinating world of Wizartry. "This is the book your aunt and uncle gave you for a present and we later found in your locker last school year! How did he get a hold of it?"

Doodles took the book from her and flipped through the pages. "I'm not sure, but the last place I remember seeing the book was when you brought it to Riddley's shop," Doodles said. "Either way, there are notes scribbled on one of the pages. Look for yourself."

He held the book up to her and she nodded.

"Why would he write on one of the pages? What is that anyway?" Darren asked, coming over to look with them.

"I'm not sure," Doodles said. "But it looks like something really ancient. Not sure why the Principal would be interested in this but if it is in this book then it has to be something to do with Wizartry or Inner Earth. I don't think I like this. The only way to know for certain is to bring the book to Riddley or my uncle and ask."

They all stared at the page, taking in the beautiful, intricately-detailed drawing. It was almost like a photograph, it was so lifelike. It was of a golden, circular object, with writing of some sort across its surface, etched neatly with fine silver. There was a ruby on top and it had several odd-looking feathers attached to it. Each feather was a different color and shape.

Laura grabbed the book and started to unzip her backpack.

"What are you doing?" Doodles asked.

"What does it look like? We have to take the book to get it checked out," she explained.

"No," Doodles said, changing his mind.

"No?" Laura paused.

"Remember, we have to keep everything the way it was. I will draw a replica of what we saw. I am very good at remembering drawings," Doodles said.

"Yeah, you should listen to him, Laura," Samantha said. "He knows what he's doing."

Laura clenched her fist. "I'm getting really sick of you," she said. "Doodles and I have been friends for years! I think I know him a whole lot better than you do."

Doodles cleared his throat awkwardly to break the tension. He grabbed the book and looked at the notes. "Look what is written here. He labeled it 'Hollyport Fine Arts Museum'. Then there are just a bunch of unimportant facts about the museum, like open hours and times."

Darren spoke up from behind them, "Wait a second. Those look like the kinds of lists my Dad makes for the workers in his factory, but this is labeled 'guard'. I think it's a schedule of security guard work shifts and rotations. What would the Mayor need those for?" he asked. He was practically standing on his tip toes to look past Laura's shoulder at the book.

Laura said," Maybe that thing in the book is at the museum and the Mayor is trying to steal it!"

She put the book back on the desk where she found it.

"Why else would he need the guard schedule?" Laura asked.

Doodles nodded. "Sounds about right for him. We have to warn Riddley and the others. We need more answers about what this thing is."

The four of them stopped. Doodles' heart skipped a beat. There were footfalls in the hallway outside. The lock on the door began to turn.

* * *

There wasn't enough time to use Wizartry or think of a solution. They had to react. The four of them dove underneath the desk and huddled together as the door opened and someone walked in. All they could see were the person's black dress shoes and suit pants. They walked toward the desk. There was a shuffling noise as something was moved aside and picked up. The figure then walked out the door, slamming it shut.

Doodles looked at his friends as they climbed out of their hiding places and then signaled for quiet.

"Who was that? Was it the Principal?" Laura asked.

"Probably," Doodles replied.

"This is intense," Samantha said. She looked really excited and Doodles was happy she was having a good time despite the nerve-wracking consequences they could have gotten into just by being in here.

Darren, who was still on his hands and knees, stood up suddenly and tapped Doodles on the shoulder. "The book!" he cried out. "It's gone!"

They all looked towards the desk top. Sure enough, Doodles' book was the only item noticeably missing.

"Let's get out of here and go see Riddley," Darren said. "We have to figure out what the Principal is planning."

"Who is Riddley?" Samantha asked.

"He is... well he's my trainer, and a very interesting man," Doodles explained. "You'll see."

They left in a hurry, none of them wanting to stay any longer than they had to. Too many close calls for one day.

"I don't know if I like her," Laura whispered to Darren, watching Samantha walk next to Doodles, smiling and making him laugh at some joke. "I don't know why Doodles trusts her so much."

Darren shrugged. "I think I can guess." He chuckled and then stopped abruptly when he saw Laura's frown. "She seems nice," Darren added awkwardly.

"So did Rita at first," Laura warned.

"Yeah, but Samantha is really pretty," Darren added.

Laura rolled her eyes and moved past Darren.

"Boys," she murmured.

# CHAPTER 5

Rita signaled and Alanso ducked behind a large row of purple bushes. Another search party of Wizarts made their way past their location. That was the third group in under an hour. They were persistent in their desire to capture Rita and Alanso, but they weren't half as clever as they needed to be to do so, Rita mused as she chuckled out loud.

"What's so funny?" Alanso snarled. "We're stuck in Inner Earth with no way of getting back and the entire Wizartry world is hunting us."

Rita laughed again. "I just thought of an idea." Her fierce eyes looked into the distance. "We will go to Loric for aid. You know what they say, 'The enemy of our enemy is our friend.'" She picked up a long centipede and crushed it between her fingers. Black paint squirted out onto the ground.

Alanso was about to protest but then thought better of it. Worst case scenario, Loric took care of Rita and he would finally be free of her. "Where will we find him?" he asked.

He shifted his weight and moaned as his knees cracked. His tall and lanky frame was not meant for all this ducking, hiding, or running.

"Let me handle that!" Rita said. "First we have to lose these search parties. I will admit that it is quite flattering to be on the

Wizartry's most wanted list. Shame I have to share that title with you."

Alanso could have sworn she smiled, but she hid it well if she did.

* * *

"Of course I know exactly what that is," Riddley said.

Darren, Laura, Samantha, and Doodles had wasted no time in getting to Riddley's shop on Lamter Lane. Riddley scratched his chin thoughtfully as he took a good look at Doodles' replica of the drawing they had seen in the book in the Principal's office. It had taken quite a lot of convincing for Riddley to allow Samantha to join them. He had put up a good fuss and then finally conceded. Doodles had saved Inner Earth before, after all, and Riddley trusted his judgment.

"Well, what is it?" Doodles asked.

Riddley shook his head.

"Been some time since I have seen it, but I still recognize it. It's an ancient and very important Wizartry artifact. It has been missing for quite a while. Why? Where did you find this?" Riddley's bushy eyebrows rose and his eyes grew serious.

"We think it may be in the Fine Arts Museum," Doodles replied, adding, "Did you know the Mayor is our school principal now? My book was in his office. I don't know how he got his hands on it, but we think he's after the artifact."

"This is not good," Riddley muttered. "There was an archeology dig a few months ago just outside of town. Maybe they uncovered it. If it falls into the wrong hands..."

"What happens?" Darren asked. "What does it do?"

Riddley took a deep breath and then said, "It is another way to get into Inner Earth. The gateway in the flower shop is the most well-known entranceway, but long ago, ancient Wizarts discovered a way to make an object that teleported the user directly into Inner Earth. They made it so they wouldn't have to make their way back to the shop every time they wanted to return to Inner Earth. Obviously this could create a security threat if it fell into the wrong hands and so the object was hidden away in a safe place and only taken out for journeys away from the usual gateway. Unfortunately, with everything that has been going on, the object was lost roughly twenty years ago."

Doodles looked to his friends. "Then we just have to get it back before Mr. Derringer gets his hand on it."

"It's not that simple, Doodles," Riddley said. "You certainly can't just waltz into the museum and steal it. You could go to jail."

"Wait!" Laura exclaimed.

Darren nearly jumped out of his shoes from the sudden sound of her voice.

"Can't you draw it?" she asked excitedly.

"Yes," Riddley said. "But when you draw a copy of it, it still wouldn't have any of the magical Wizartry properties. It wouldn't work."

They all stood there in thoughtful quiet for a while.

"But you can draw an object that looks exactly like it?" Darren asked.

"Pretty close, yeah," Doodles replied.

"Well, then how about you draw it and we sneak it into the museum and replace the real one with the fake one? How can they accuse us of stealing if it doesn't look like it's missing?" Darren asked.

Riddley clapped. "Very good idea, Darren."

"We'll have to move soon," Darren said. "The Mayor could try to make his move at any time."

"We'll go right after school tomorrow and check it out," Doodles said.

"Wait," Laura said. "You are talking about stealing something regardless if you are replacing it with a fake. It's not only morally wrong, it's illegal. We could all go to jail."

Samantha frowned. "I guess I agree with her on this one, Doodles. Isn't it wrong to steal?"

Laura looked at Samantha in surprise. She wasn't sure if she was being sincere and didn't know if she even wanted her support in this. She still hadn't figured out Samantha, yet.

"Sometimes we must do things to prevent worse actions," Riddley said. "Think about it. If we don't steal this, the entire Wizartry world could be destroyed."

There was a moment of silence and then Laura said, "I suppose you're right. It just feels wrong to me."

Samantha looked towards Doodles. "What do you think, Doodles?"

All eyes were on Doodles. He straightened his shoulders and held his chin up high. "Let's come up with another plan. I can't go through with something so wrong. Let's at least go down to the museum and check it out. Maybe it will help us come up with another idea."

\* \* \*

The school bell rang signaling the end of art class. Mrs. Roberts stood up from her desk and approached the students as they began to pack up. "Real quick, before I forget," Mrs. Roberts said. She grabbed some papers off of her desk. "These are permission slips for a field trip we will be taking on Thursday. I know this is short notice, but I need them signed and returned by tomorrow morning."

Each student grabbed one paper from her as they left, leaving Doodles and Samantha as the last ones to leave. He grabbed the paper and thanked her. He was about to stuff it into his backpack to look at later when he caught a glimpse of the field trip destination: the Fine Arts Museum of Hollyport. Doodles couldn't believe it. Maybe it was just a coincidence.

When they were in the hallway, safe from Mrs. Roberts' overhearing, Doodles whispered to Samantha, "Do you see where the field trip is to? I can't believe it."

She nodded. They slowly began walking down the hall.

"Hey, Doodles. Can I ask you something?"

"Sure, of course," Doodles replied.

"Why do you hang out with Laura and Darren?" Samantha asked. "No offense, but you could do much better than them."

Doodles didn't know what to say. He didn't expect that from her. Laura and Darren had been his best friends for years.

"What do you mean?" Doodles asked.

"It's just that with your powers, you could be the most popular kid in school. I could help make that happen," she suggested.

Doodles wanted to say "yes" so badly. She was so beautiful and he had always wanted to be one of the popular kids. Imagine all the fun he could have.

He shook his head to clear it. No, that wasn't who he was. He was a good person and a loyal friend. "I can't do that," Doodles said.

"Fine, suit yourself," Samantha said, giving him a disappointed look. They continued on in silence together.

It didn't take long for them to find Laura in the hallway. She was talking to a friend, but when Doodles and Samantha approached and motioned to her, she said goodbye to her friend and came over.

"What is it?" she asked.

"Look," Doodles said, holding up the field trip permission form. Laura looked it over and then gasped.

"Do you think your teacher is in on it?" Laura asked.

"I don't know. She seems so nice, but it's so hard to trust anybody these days," Doodles said.

Suddenly there was a voice behind Doodles that made him jump in surprise. "Oh, good. I caught you before you went home."

It was Mrs. Roberts.

Doodles wasn't sure how long she had been standing there and what, if anything, she had overheard. "What do you mean?" Doodles asked.

"I just wanted to tell you how happy I am with your progress in only a few days! You really are talented! I'm excited to see what else you can create in my class." She clapped enthusiastically. "I hope you are enjoying this class, Doodles! A lot of fun things are coming your way!" She gave a warm smile and then walked off down the hallway toward the faculty lounge.

Laura looked at Doodles. "I can't tell if she's sincere or not. Maybe she doesn't know anything and is being used by the Principal."

Doodles shrugged. "I hope you're right, but either way, I'll let you know if she says anything new tomorrow after the permission slips are all turned in."

Samantha said, "I'm going too, obviously."

Laura ignored her and leaned in to Doodles and whispered, "Are we still sticking to the plan to check the museum out?"

Doodles thought for a moment. "Let's go check it out. I don't want to take any chances. If things look good, we can do it."

"I have to get home," Samantha said to them. "I'll see you all later."

Doodles thought it best not to mention anything that Samantha had talked to him about in the school hallway. It was

27

better not to stir up any trouble, especially if Samantha was going to be hanging around more often. Maybe it hadn't been the best idea to trust her so soon with Wizartry, but it was too late to turn back now. Hopefully she would come around to his friends. He wanted them all to get along. He would have to show her that they were good people.

Laura and Doodles walked off the school grounds after finding Darren. They stopped by Riddley's shop on Lamter Lane before heading to the museum. Riddley let Darren and Laura paint some of the blank canvases hung up on several easels while they talked. They stopped by because not a one of them wasn't nervous about going to the museum. Riddley's talk and the act of painting momentarily eased the tension and apprehension. They were on their way with only a few warnings about being careful. Doodles knew Riddley really cared about him.

"Things are never simple," Laura said as they walked. "I'm always so impressed with you, Doodles," she said. "We will figure this all out with you leading." She smiled at him.

Doodles nodded and tried to act like the leader she thought he was.

"Let's do this," Doodles said.

# CHAPTER 6

D oodles had never been to Hollyport's Fine Arts Museum before. His parents had asked him to go a few times, but he had always been busy with one thing or another. Doodles didn't particularly like museums. He enjoyed drawing, but staring at artifacts and old paintings wasn't that much fun for him. He liked to be the one to create things. When Doodles asked, Laura and Darren both said they had never been there before, either.

They approached the stately building and looked up at the large white columns across its front. There was a wide set of stairs that could easily hold all the students from the middle school for a group picture. The stairs led up to a humongous set of wooden, double doors. There were a few people going in and out but not an overwhelming amount.

They made their way up the stairs. "Just act normal," Doodles said.

"I thought I was, until you said that. Now I don't know how to act normal. What do I do with my hands?" Darren asked.

Laura laughed. "Just keep them at your sides. Don't touch anything and stick with us."

Doodles marveled at how Darren had moments of confidence and moments of nervousness. He seemed to be figuring it out and he hoped they would see a lot more of the confident

Darren. As of now, it was so unpredictable how Darren would react that it made Doodles somewhat uneasy.

Doodles looked around to see if there was anyone he might know and then they made their way through the doorway. The ceiling inside was tall, similar to when Doodles had gone on a family vacation to Grand Central Station in New York City. Then and now, Doodles stood there in awe, taking in the enormity of the building. He wished he had agreed to come with his parents so he could have seen this sooner.

"Wow," Laura said.

"Yeah, tell me about it," Darren said. "This place is awesome!"

"It sure is, but remember why we're here. Stay focused," Doodles said.

* * *

There was a short line to purchase museum tickets. As they waited in line, Doodles took the opportunity to look around.

There were only two security guards that he could see in the main room. But the main room didn't matter so much. The success of their plan depended on surveying the room with the Wizart artifact. Doodles wasn't even sure which room it was in. They would have to go room by room and see what sort of security the museum had in place, and determine how accessible the artifact would be. He was thankful he'd decided on the right choice of not attempting to swap the real artifact with a replica. Besides. The artifact was most likely in a sealed container or behind glass, and he and his friends weren't exactly expert thieves.

After paying for the tickets, they began to explore the museum. They made an effort to make it look like they were interested in other exhibits in case someone noticed them. It may have been overly cautious, but they had all agreed on the walk over that being careful about this was the way to go.

The next room was filled with paintings from the Renaissance era. Two of them Doodles recognized from his history text books. *The Creation of Adam* was more awe inspiring in person and Doodles found himself looking closely to see if the man and the God depicted there were actually touching hands or if they were separated by only an inch. If they were separated, Doodles wondered if the artist was trying to convey that the spiritual world was always just out of reach. Then there was the *Mona Lisa*, hanging in the center of the far wall. Doodles knew about the debate over whether she was smiling or not. To Doodles, and perhaps because of his own perspective on life, he thought it was clear right away that she was smiling. Doodles would have been impressed by the rest of the paintings on display just a few years ago, but after seeing the marvels of Wizartry, these others seemed paltry in comparison.

Doodles noted that there was only one museum attendant in this room. He felt a sense of guilt and doubt creep into his conscious as he realized what they had thought about doing which would have been not only illegal but also morally reprehensible. He strained his brain to try to justify his original plans by attempting to understand the bigger picture, the ultimate goal of saving all of Wizartry. Doodles felt bad, but knew that they had ultimately come to the right decision and for that, he could learn to get over his momentary lapse in judgment.

After moving through four large rooms, the group came to another one that was kept rather dark except for a few lights pointed downward into the center of the room. In the center was a marble pedestal. On the pedestal was the Wizartry artifact encased in a glass box. The glass looked thick and was bolted into the pedestal with large screws. There were two attendants in this room and they looked anything but bored. They stood at attention liked trained watchdogs, eying their surroundings.

"Figures," Laura whispered.

They knew better than to linger too long in this room but Doodles wanted to get a closer look. When they were right next to the artifact, Doodles sighed. Even seeing it this close didn't give him any other ideas. He needed to figure out another solution, and quick.

Doodles looked around the room. He could have sworn he saw Boogley walk past one of the paintings. It would be like him to follow Doodles on an adventure even if Doodles had told him to stay home. The citizens of Hollyport, the non-Wizarts, would scream if they saw him. The creature had been created by Doodles' imagination, and Boogley was full of curiosity and even fuller of stubbornness. It was entirely within the realm of possibility that he was here. If Boogley had been there, though, Doodles couldn't locate him. His friends seemed so distracted by the artifact, glowing brilliantly in the center of the room. He followed their gaze and shifted his focus to the artifact.

There was a gold-colored plaque on the side of the pedestal that stated this was an unknown artifact from an unknown era dug up in a recent excavation at an archeology dig site fairly close to Hollyport. Doodles looked up and saw that the two museum guards were watching them. They didn't approach, but it still made Doodles feel uneasy.

"Let's go," Doodles whispered. He felt that the museum attendants' eyes were judging them. Doodles wanted to be anywhere but in this room.

* * *

The three friends hurried to Riddley's shop. It was late, but Riddley was always there late.

"I doubt Mr. Derringer will try to steal the artifact during the day," Darren said. "He'll have to use tools to get it out and there are too many people around."

"Unless there is someone on the inside helping him out," Laura chimed in.

"What do you mean?" Doodles asked.

Laura replied, "He bribed police officers before. Maybe he has someone on the inside of the museum or in the town. Or, he has someone with Wizartry powers helping him, like Alanso or Rita."

"Then why go through the trouble of becoming a school principal? Why make an art class?" Darren asked.

She shrugged. "I don't know."

They stood in silence for a few moments until Riddley cleared his throat. "It's getting late. There's nothing we can do right now. Go home and get some rest. We may have to wait and see what happens on the field trip."

"What if he makes a move before then?" Darren asked. "Shouldn't we alert the museum or the police?"

Riddley paused in thought and then said, "Yes. I suppose we have no choice but to tell the police about our suspicions. Careful about what details we provide to them. Obviously nothing about Wizartry."

Doodles wanted to protest at first, but Riddley was right. He hadn't thought of any other option and he had a feeling they were running out of time. Hopefully the police would help, but Doodles and his friends really didn't have anything solid on Mr. Derringer. He knew enough about law from his father that the evidence they did have was circumstantial. It was extremely frustrating."

"Any word on how the Wizarts in Inner Earth are doing trying to find and capture Rita or Alanso yet?" Doodles asked, hopeful to get some sort of good news.

Riddley shook his head. "No, but they have them on the run in Inner Earth. You will be one of the first to know when they are found. We have every available Wizart searching. It's only a matter of time."

Too much waiting and uncertainty was starting to stress Doodles out. Maybe the walk to the police station would clear his head.

"Time to go," Doodles said.

# CHAPTER 7

Alanso and Rita stood in front of the entrance to Loric's cave. They had narrowly escaped numerous Wizartry search parties. Rita had to admit they were persistent. Several of the Wizarts had drawn spyglasses and had spotted Alanso and Rita a few times. At night time they drew large search lights and shined them all about.

Rita was running out of ways to avoid capture. She had drawn several hiding places and each time had come close to being discovered. She and Alanso were more skillful than most of the Wizarts who were after them, but the Wizarts had numbers on their side. Each group that came after them was made up of six Wizarts. They were more organized than Rita would have thought. Council Member Charles was probably overseeing their capture. He was meticulous with details and well organized. He probably wanted their capture most of all. After being kidnapped last year by Rita, revenge was undoubtedly on his mind.

As the eldest of the Wizartry council members, fast approaching eighty years of age, Charles remembered an era when the Wizarts were more organized and followed the rules more closely. People like Charles were on their way out though, Rita mused. He probably wanted the recognition of their capture before he retired. Silly old man. With Loric's help, no one could stand in their way.

They entered Loric's cave. Even Alanso at six and a half feet tall did not have to duck as the cave was made for a giant. Alanso marveled how such a tiny woman as Rita could walk into the darkness of a giant's cave with nerves of steel. He hid his fear well, but Rita seemed completely relaxed.

She took out her paint brush from a bag slung over her shoulder and drew a lantern. Holding it up, she led them deep into the cave.

It seemed to go on for miles. There were paintings on the walls, all done in dark blue paint. The paintings seemed to depict different times in Wizartry history. It showed pictures of ancient Wizartry council meetings, the Great Exile, the Inauguration of the First Council, and many other important moments.

A deep voice sounded from behind them. "You are brave to come before me without my permission."

"Or foolish," Alanso whispered.

Loric stepped into the light of the lantern, towering over them with his massive frame. The blue tattoos running across Loric's entire body glowed brightly in the dim light. Alanso noted that Loric's sinewy muscles looked tense, probably ready to snap them in half if the mood suited him.

He waved his hands and the drawings on the cave wall began to glow brighter, the entire cave now lit in an eerie blue glow.

"Why do you come here?" Loric demanded, his voice a deep rumble reverberating off of the cave walls. Alanso wasn't sure how far the cave went, but from the echo it sounded like many more miles.

"We want to make you a deal," Rita said.

* * *

Riddley had insisted that the kids were on their own at the police station. Doodles tried to convince Riddley to come, but Riddley kept mentioning a vague dislike for police and that he didn't want them to know his face. Doodles didn't want to press him too hard.

They were sitting at a long, wooden table in one of the interrogation rooms with a bored-looking policeman.

"So you're saying the former Mayor of Hollyport, one of the most popular people in the entire town, is trying to steal an artifact from the museum?" The policeman looked skeptical. "You are either playing a prank on us or are looking for trouble where there is none."

Laura responded first. "Can't you at least bring him in for questioning?"

"No," the policeman said. "No, I certainly cannot. We can't just bring people in for questioning about a crime that hasn't even been committed and with no evidence other than the word of three kids. I'm sorry, but no. If you don't have anything else, I have to get through a lot of paperwork today." He motioned to the door.

Doodles saw that his friends were looking toward him for their next move. Only, there wasn't a next move. They had told all the facts, leaving out only the Wizartry parts. If the police wouldn't help them, they would have to wait to see Mr. Derringer's next move.

\* \* \*

"Doodles. Doodles!" Mr. Lanhorn yelled out.

"Huh?" Doodles said, looking up from idly twirling his spaghetti with his fork.

"Are you paying attention?" his father asked.

"Sorry, no," Doodles admitted. "I'm just so overwhelmed with everything going on."

Mrs. Lanhorn came over and rubbed Doodles' back. "We understand, sweetie." She smiled down at him. He resisted the urge to squirm. He was in eighth grade now and didn't need his mother babying him. At the same time, however, with everything going on, it was nice to feel loved.

"I was saying," his father continued. "Your uncle has made the Wizartry Council aware of the former Mayor's scheme. While most of the Wizarts are searching for Alanso and Rita, they want to make reclaiming the Wizartry artifact a priority as well."

"That's good news," Doodles said.

"Yes, yes it is," Mr. Lanhorn said.

"That means you kids won't have to deal with this alone. In fact, the Wizartry Council wants to meet with you immediately to come up with a plan."

"Are you coming with me?" Doodles asked. He did not like going in front of the Council by himself. They were rather intimidating sometimes.

His father shook his head. "No, but they want you to bring Laura, Samantha, and Darren."

Doodles' father took his car keys out of his pocket and placed them on the kitchen table.

"Please finish your dinner, and then call your friends and tell them we'll be picking them up," he said. "Right away."

* * *

Darren and Laura had walked through the Wizartry Council chamber before when it was empty. Samantha had never been there. The chamber stood deep under the basement of the flower shop and it held the gateway to Inner Earth. The florist in the shop was actually the gatekeeper there to make sure only Wizarts and their rarely invited guests gained entry to the portal that led to the Council chamber and on to Inner Earth. Now, the three large chairs were filled with the three Wizartry Council members, Holly, Charles, and Brian. Each of them had donned their ceremonial Wizartry robes and hats. The three iron molded lanterns in the room were lit.

Doodles noted that, unlike the time of his first of three tests, the spectator rows were empty. Council members Holly and Charles nodded toward Doodles, with Holly even going so far as to smile.

Brian, however, gave Doodles a menacing stare. Doodles still wasn't sure why Brian didn't like him. Since the first day he had met Brian, the man looked down on him with a snobby attitude, even saying that Doodles was too young to participate in the tests. It was not a good feeling to know someone hated him, yet not knowing why they felt that way.

"I didn't want you on this mission," Council Member Brian stated. "In fact, I don't think it's a good idea for a relatively untrained candidate for a Wizart title, to be on any mission, especially one so important. So far you have been lucky, but three times is not always the charm. However, my colleagues seem to think we have no choice but to use you."

Holly smiled, waving her hand dismissively at Brian. "That's not entirely true," she said. "Yes, Doodles, we need to use you, but Charles and I feel you have proven yourself time and time again, and that is not a matter of luck, it is pure talent, intelligence, and knowing when to ask for the help of friends."

Charles cleared his throat. "We have been briefed on the situation. Your enrollment in the art class and your Wizartry skills make you invaluable. You are our inside man."

Darren and Laura fidgeted. They felt awkward being talked about and yet not being addressed directly, and they weren't sure where they fit into all of this. Samantha was standing quietly. It was all so new to her.

Holly noticed them and smiled. "Your friends really are important to this mission, Doodles."

Doodles looked at his friends. Although they stood there uncertainly, they were much more confident than they had been last year when all of this started. Samantha seemed to be holding up okay.

"How can we help?" Darren asked.

Laura added, "Yeah, just let us know what we need to do and we'll do it." It was Doodles' turn to smile, much to the chagrin of Council Member Brian. It felt so good to know that his friends always had his back.

Holly continued, "We have been made aware of the Museum field trip on Thursday. Upon further investigating, it seems that the entire school is going. We, the Wizartry Council, feel that if the Mayor is going to attempt to steal the artifact, it would make sense that he uses the crowd of students as a distraction. You will need your friends to assist. We can only spare a few Wizarts as most are searching for Alanso and Rita, so everyone we can enlist will be helpful."

"I'm still not quite sure what you want us to do," Doodles said.

Charles said, "As we speak, we have two Wizarts, in addition to the museum's guards, watching the artifact within the museum."

"We didn't see them there," Darren blurted out.

"Don't worry," Charles replied. "They are there, even if you can't see them.

"I need you four to be extra eyes, ready to call security or stop the Mayor yourself if need be. We cannot let him get hold of the artifact."

"But we can't watch it forever," Doodles said.

"No, we can't," Charles responded. "That is why the Council is working on a way to get it back into proper hands."

"How?" asked Doodles.

Brian gave Doodles a nasty look. "You needn't concern yourself with our affairs. Just do what you are told to do."

Doodles wanted to say something smart back but he didn't want to start trouble. There were bigger issues to deal with currently.

# CHAPTER 8

A lanso waited in the getaway car. He gripped the steering wheel of the beige Toyota Camry with tightened fists. If there was one thing Alanso hated more than Rita or Doodles, it was waiting.

He had the car parallel parked across the street from the Hollyport Fine Arts Museum. They had to find a car with a sunroof since Loric was nearly ten feet tall. They would have been quite the scene driving down the streets if people could see Loric as he really looked.

The Wizarts would be after them again in numbers as soon as they learned that Alanso, Rita and Loric had escaped Inner Earth by forcing their way through two search parties and ten Wizarts guarding the entrance to Inner Earth at the base of the flower shop.

....They needed to grab the artifact and get out quick. Even Loric couldn't stand against the might of the police and the Wizarts in a large group.

Inside the museum, Loric and Rita approached the ticket counter. Loric's talents as an ancient, founding Wizart were very strong and different from the other modern day Wizarts. He had the amazing ability to make people see things differently than they actually were. Even though he towered over all others, at this moment people saw him as an old man with a grizzled beard. The few visitors standing around parted quickly for them as Rita shoved her way to the ticket counter.

The woman at the ticket counter tried her best to act casual as Rita leaned over the counter with a menacing stare. Rita smirked with pleasure at the woman's discomfort.

"Two tickets," Rita demanded. She handed the ticket woman a crumpled up twenty dollar bill and laughed heartily. "Keep your petty change," she said. The woman handed Rita two tickets with a trembling hand. Rita had to admit that this woman was braver than most to have not run from her.

Loric made his way into the next room with Rita following close behind. Rita and Alanso had made a deal with Loric. They agreed to get the artifact for him if he helped them to make their way out of Inner Earth and back to Hollyport.

He walked into the artifact room. There was only a young couple pushing a stroller and two museum attendants. Loric had to wait patiently until the couple left so he could drop the illusion spell. Being patient was not easy for Loric, but the less people, the less likely more guards would come to stop them before they got away. There was no need for the illusion spell any more. The two stunned museum attendants shifted nervously, their hands moving closer to the Tasers that hung at their sides when the spell wore off.

Loric laughed, his voice echoing across the room. He walked with confidence over to the artifact and took a full swing with his right arm, his fist shattering the glass as if it were just a party piñata. Alarms went off throughout the museum.

Just as Loric reached for the artifact, his body shook. Looking down, Loric noticed with annoyance that one of the guards had used his stun gun on him. Much to that guard's dismay, Loric looked more annoyed than hurt.

Loric ignored the Taser and grabbed hold of the artifact. The tattoos on his body glowed brightly as another Taser from the second guard went into his back. The second one caused him to wince in pain, but it also made him angry.

He turned to face the guards and gave such a howl of rage that the two guards ran out of the room nearly falling over each other to get out.

Loric and Rita turned to leave before the real police came when a voice called out, "Stop!"

Looking behind them, figuring another useless security guard was trying to be a hero, Rita was surprised to see two Wizarts standing there. So the Council wasn't as dumb and useless as she thought.

The Wizarts, whom Rita did not recognize, approached cautiously, their paint brushes held out. They both began to paint. Clearly, they were skilled. The Council had sent two who were powerful.

Loric charged. Just before he reached the newcomers, a stone wall appeared and Loric ran into it with such force that he bounced back and fell to the floor. The wall was well made and held. Whoever these men were, they were trained and prepared. They had obviously been sent to guard the artifact.

Rita could see the Wizarts were prepared to stop a giant, but they had no idea who she was or what she could do. The Wizarts were clearly trying to stall until the police came, a situation Rita wanted to avoid. She approached the wall and laughed as she painted a doorway in the wall before the Wizarts on the other side of the wall could see what she was doing and react.

"After you," she said as she opened the door. Loric charged through and the sound of a loud thump could be heard as Loric crashed into the Wizarts from the other side. It made her giggle. The Wizarts were not ready for Loric to get through the wall that quickly. She poured dissolving ink on the rest of the wall as she and Loric ran out with the artifact, and Rita felt like they made quite the pair.

* * *

Alanso sped off down the road. He looked in the rear view mirror several times. No one was following them yet. Loric, his head through the sunroof, and Rita both sat in the backseat, staring outside in quiet. Alanso chuckled to himself. The three of them were a powerful combination.

Alanso swallowed nervously. The original plan was going well, but his own plan was yet to come to fruition. He didn't make eye contact with Rita. She always seemed to read him like she had some sort of psychic power. He knew that wasn't true, but she was perceptive and cunning and he didn't want to take any chances with her finding out what he was planning.

He pulled off the road and onto a dirt path. It wound through a small forest heading east. He turned on his high beams. The forest was eerily silent, their car the only car for as far as he could see. The dirt behind their speeding car flew upward in a cloud.

"Slow down," Rita said. "No one is after us and you're going to run into a tree if you take those turns at the speed you're going." She didn't raise her voice. She just said it in a command, expecting Alanso to follow without question. He hated her so much right now. She always got her way, but that would change soon enough.

They came to a log cabin. Alanso pulled the car in and they all hopped out. The lights in the cabin were off. It was dark and the crickets chirped loudly from within the woods.

"Stick to the plan," Rita said. "Loric and I get in one car and you get in the other," she said, pointing to the two other cars parked by the cabin. "Take the artifact with you like we talked about," Rita said. Without waiting for any questions or reply, Rita and Loric hopped into one of the new cars and sped off.

Alanso breathed a sigh of relief. This was going better than he could have ever hoped for. Instead of getting into the other car, Alanso went up the steps to the front door of the cabin and knocked.

A few moments passed and then the lights in the cabin turned on. The cabin door swung open with a load creak.

"About time," Mr. Derringer said. "I don't like waiting."

Alanso smiled.

"Well, where is it?" Mr. Derringer asked with excitement.

Alanso took out the artifact from his bag and passed it to the Mayor.

Mr. Derringer's eyes lit up. "This will give me so much power!" He held it closer to his face. "Look at the detail on it. Fantastic!"

Alanso cleared his throat.

Mr. Derringer put the artifact into his own bag and said, "Ah, I take it you want your payment?" He walked back into the living room of the cabin and grabbed a duffel bag off of the couch. "Three hundred thousand, just as promised."

Alanso grabbed the bag.

"Wait," Mr. Derringer said. "I have to ask you. I thought you and Rita were close friends. Haven't you worked with her for a long time now? I am curious, why the betrayal?"

Alanso's face grew red with anger. "That woman never appreciated me! She bossed me around, made me feel insignificant, and never delivered on her promises. I have been trying to plan something against her but she was always one step ahead of me. Not this time. I am tired of all the secrecy of Wizartry. I want to live well and not have to hide what I have. This money will help me do that."

"I see," Mr. Derringer replied. "Well, come on in. I need your skill to replicate the artifact. I'm just an amateur when it comes to Wizartry."

"My pleasure," Alanso said.

He couldn't stop grinning thinking of Rita's face when she realized he had betrayed her.

\* \* \*

Detective Lawrence O'Malley of the Hollyport police department shook his head in disbelief. This was the fifth time he had reviewed the security footage from the museum robbery. In fifteen years of service, he had never seen anything like it. O'Malley had seen tall people before, even some nearing seven feet tall, but from the footage verifying the eye witness accounts, the man was almost ten feet tall.

There were no tools used, just brute force. After the giant man grabbed the museum artifact, the screen turned to static. The museum security guards said that the Tasers hadn't even fazed the robber. Maybe one Taser had malfunctioned and didn't discharge a shock, but both of them malfunctioning at the same time was against the odds. There was also a woman with the robber. Whether she was an accomplice or not, Detective O'Malley's team was already scanning facial recognition software on both. So far, no matches, which was not a good sign.

"O'Malley! In my office! Now!" The Chief of Police stuck his head out of the office long enough to yell and then went back to his desk.

Detective O'Malley sighed. He took his time getting up. Let the boss wait a few extra seconds.

There wasn't much crime in Hollyport. With nothing else sitting on his desk, this pushed the museum up to a priority. The chief was probably getting pressure from the museum chairman to solve it as soon as possible.

"Sit down," the chief said. O'Malley took a seat in the uncomfortable wooden chair across from the chief's desk.

"Tell me you have an update or a lead," the chief started before O'Malley could say anything. "The longer this goes on, the more likely these thieves are to skip town and sell the artifact on the black market. Well?" He gave O'Malley an expectant look.

"Facial recognition has not come up with anything, Sir," O'Malley admitted. He preferred to be honest and blunt instead of beating around the bush. Besides, the chief was a good read of people. "The man who did this should be easily spotted at almost ten feet tall. We put out descriptions of him and of his suspected accomplice. We have all available units scouring the town."

"I want results," the chief said.

"You don't think I do?" O'Malley said and then regretted talking back. "Sorry, Boss. Just been a rough week."

The police chief's eyes narrowed. "I don't want to hear excuses. What leads do you have? There has to be something."

O'Malley strained his brain. He had already interviewed all eye witnesses. Then a sudden thought came to him. "There might be something," he said.

"Well?"

O'Malley sighed. It wasn't much, but it might get the chief off his back for the time being. "This may be a stretch, but I reviewed the footage for the last week. I focused on the actual room the artifact was in. There were three kids who visited the room for an unusual amount of time. Now that I think of it, it stands out because they hurried through every other room they went into. It was like they were deliberately looking for that one artifact. It didn't cross my mind that they could be involved since they are just kids, but maybe, and this is a strong maybe, the thieves used the kids to do some reconnaissance."

There were a few moments of silence as the chief mulled it over. "It's a stretch," he said. "Find out who these kids are and interrogate them. You'll have to have their parents present because they're minors. Let me know right away."

O'Malley nodded. "I'm on it, Sir."

* * *

Detective O'Malley knocked on the door. The house was plain looking, pretty much the same as every other house in the neighborhood. Nothing seemed out of the ordinary. There was a sound of footsteps on the other side of the door, floorboards creaking.

"Can I help you?" a man asked, opening the door a crack.

"Mr. Lanhorn?" O'Malley asked.

"Yes?" Mr. Lanhorn replied, keeping the door barely open a crack.

"I'm Detective O'Malley from the Hollyport Police Department. I wanted to ask your son a few questions regarding the recent robbery at Hollyport Fine Arts Museum. You may be present during our talk. May I come in?"

There was a moment of hesitation and then Mr. Lanhorn swung the door open. "You are welcome to talk to him, but I don't see what he has to do with a robbery."

O'Malley followed Doodles' father inside. Once in the living room, Mr. Lanhorn pointed to the couch. "He's upstairs. I'll go get him."

O'Malley took the opportunity to look around. The house seemed as ordinary as you could get. Then again, sometimes the ordinary ones were hiding something.

Mr. Lanhorn came downstairs with his son. "Now remember," Mr. Lanhorn spoke loud enough that Doodles and O'Malley could hear him. "You don't have to answer any questions you don't feel comfortable answering."

O'Malley gave Doodles a friendly smile. "You're not in any trouble, kid. Just need some information."

Doodles sat down on the opposite side of the couch. Mr. Lanhorn stood with arms crossed. Doodles was nervous. The more he tried to act casual, the more he felt he looked suspect. He kept wondering if he looked like he was acting natural with his hands and the more he thought about it, the more awkward he felt.

"So, have you been to the museum lately?" O'Malley asked.

Doodles knew it would be pointless to deny it. It was a casual question meant to catch him in a lie. "Yes," Doodles responded.

"Go there often?" O'Malley continued with the line of questions.

Doodles shrugged. "No, not often. It was my first time there."

O'Malley nodded. "I see. Find anything interesting?"

"Not really," Doodles said. He did not like where this was inevitably heading. This detective, whoever he was, was pretty sharp.

Detective O'Malley took out a piece of paper from his coat pocket. He handed it to Doodles. "You see that artifact? You seemed pretty interested in it. In fact, you spent most of your time in that room alone staring at that one piece."

Doodles swallowed nervously. He couldn't tell this detective anything that would reveal Wizartry. "It was interesting looking," Doodles admitted. "What's wrong with being interested in an artifact?"

O'Malley smirked. "Must have been real interesting."

Doodles didn't like this man. His eyes seemed to look right through him, a piercing, knowing look. He was intelligent and suspicious and he knew Doodles was hiding something.

"I guess I just found that artifact interesting," Doodles said and realized too late that he was repeating himself. "The plaque on the glass caught my eye. I've always been interested in archeology and really like the mystery of old things." Detective O'Malley nodded and grinned, slipping his hand into his coat pocket, and holding onto a piece of paper as he talked.

"Of course you do," the detective said. "It's a very unusual piece." His eyes studied Doodles. "Do you recognize either of these two people?" He held up the picture for Doodles to see.

Doodles nearly jumped off the couch as the detective held up a picture of Rita and Loric. It was too late to act casual. Doodles was sure the detective had seen his reaction, but nonetheless, he had to lie. There was no way to reasonably explain how he knew them.

"No... Never seen them. I was just surprised because they looked scary, and that man is so tall and tattooed," Doodles lied. It made him feel terrible, lying to a police officer. He wanted to leave the room, to get far away from this man and his questions.

Detective O'Malley smiled like a fisherman reeling in a big catch. "Sure, kid. Whatever you say. I'm sure we'll be in touch very soon." He stood up and gave a mock salute to Doodles' father. Detective O'Malley handed his card to Doodles' father before he left.

Mr. Lanhorn slammed the door and turned to his son after him. "This is not good."

\* \* \*

Later that night, Doodles was about to call Laura from the phone on the kitchen counter when it rang. He picked it up with a shaky hand.

"Hello?" Doodles asked.

"Doodles, it's me!" Laura said. Before he could reply or tell her what had happened with the detective she blurted out, "A detective came to my house and asked me a ton of questions! I told him I didn't know anything. He was scary, Doodles!"

Doodles said, "Calm down. The same thing happened to me earlier. I was just about to call you and tell you before you beat me to it."

"He must have talked to Darren, too. What are we going to do?" Laura asked. She sounded very scared over the phone and Doodles felt bad for her. He had brought her in to this mess.

There was a moment of silence on both ends of the phone. "Call Darren and come over," Doodles finally said. "We are going to come up with a plan to deal with this like we always do." He was just as nervous as his friend, but he also knew in the back of his mind that he and his friends could overcome anything when they worked together. "We just can't let them find out about Wizartry."

"I'm on my way," Laura said.

Doodles hung up the phone and turned around. Through the front window, Doodles saw a parked van across the street pull out and drive off. He shook his head. He was probably just being paranoid. It was a coincidence. His parents always told him he had such an active imagination.

His father was in the living room just getting off of a phone call on his cell phone. "Uncle Roger says you need to see Riddley tomorrow. He has your third and final test for you to become a Wizart."

Doodles plopped down on the couch and waited for his friends. Sometimes it seemed like the whole world rested on his shoulders. He had to get the artifact back from a deranged Wizart and a powerful giant, get the police detective off of his back, catch the Mayor with hard evidence, survive the eighth grade, and pass his final Wizartry test.

He looked up at his father, who was smiling at him.

"What?" Doodles asked.

"I'm proud of you," Mr. Lanhorn said.

Doodles smiled in turn. Maybe it wouldn't be so bad after all.

* * *

Back at the station, Detective O'Malley walked into his boss' office. He knew the chief would be there at this hour. The man always worked late.

"Well?" the chief asked.

"They know something and they're scared," O'Malley said.

"You sure?" the chief asked.

"We got a warrant to tap the phone line based off of my interviews with the kids. Yes, I'm sure," O'Malley replied.

The chief nodded. "Good work. Finally some sort of lead. Did they say anything that will help the case?"

"Wizartry," O'Malley said.

"Wizartry?" The chief put down a paper he was looking over.

"We don't know what it means yet," O'Malley explained. "Maybe it's a person, maybe a code name for the robbery mission, maybe nothing. But we are going to find out. That much I can promise you."

"Excellent job, O'Malley. Give me a follow up as soon as you find out more. I want you to stay on top of this. Take Snyder and Williams if you need more help," the chief said and without another word or even a nod, he went back to looking over reports. The man was a workhorse.

"Goodnight," O'Malley said, and left.

# CHAPTER 9

On his bike ride to Riddley's shop on Lamter Lane, Doodles could swear the van driving slowly behind him was the same van he saw the previous night. It was difficult to tell, though, as it had been very dark last night. Today, however, it was clear in the broad daylight that the van was unmarked and driving suspiciously slowly behind him. Maybe he was being overly cautious and the van was just lost or looking for a house.

Deciding to test his feelings of paranoia, Doodles started pedaling faster and making seemingly random turns. Indeed, the van sped up to keep pace and followed every turn.

This was no coincidence. Someone was following him. He quickly turned down an alleyway too small to fit the van and sped off. Behind him he heard the van screech to a halt.

By the time he reached Riddley's shop, he was sweating profusely and his heart raced. There was no sign of the van but it had been very upsetting. Did the van have to do with the detective? Was it one of the Mayor's men? Doodles hopped off of his bike and decided it would be best to get into the safety of the shop quickly.

Before he got to the door a hand grabbed his shirt and spun him around, his bike falling to the ground.

"Look who we got here," a kid with black hair and a rotund face said. Doodles knew him. Ricky always bothered him at school. "Where you going?" He kept his grip on Doodles' shirt. When he tried to back away, Ricky's grip held him in place.

"I'm just walking around," Doodles said. He wanted to use Wizartry, but he knew he couldn't. It was so frustrating not to be able to protect himself when he was more than capable of doing so.

"You need to get a life," Ricky said, and laughed at him. He let go and gave Doodles a big shove. Doodles flew back a few steps and nearly fell over backwards.

"I'll see you at school," Ricky said and gave a fake smile. He began to walk away.

Doodles didn't want to wait in case Ricky came back. He reached down to retrieve his bike, and then pushed it over to Riddley's shop.

He knocked three times and waited for the door to swing open on its own accord.

In the middle of the room Riddley was waiting as usual in his uncomfortable looking wooden chair.

He stood up when Doodles scrambled inside with his bike.

"What's wrong?" Riddley asked.

Doodles didn't even bother to tell Riddley about Ricky. Riddley couldn't do anything anyways, and besides, the van that followed him was far scarier than a bully. Doodles peeked through the store windows at the street. "I was being followed!" He exclaimed.

Riddley frowned. "By whom?" he said, glancing out the window as well.

"I'm not sure. Could have been anyone," Doodles replied. Doodles put his bike against the inside wall and sat down. His heart rate was beating a mile a minute.

Riddley sighed. "You will need to be more careful from here on out. Wizartry has too many enemies these days." He shook his head. "But let's focus on your training for now. As you know, the entire Wizartry world is looking for Loric and Rita. We have to get the artifact back. Having access to Inner Earth whenever they want is not something we can allow."

Doodles nodded. "What do you want me to do?"

Riddley smiled. "You have the heart and spirit of a true Wizart. The Wizartry Council has advised me that your final test will be to retrieve the artifact."

Doodles head slumped. The task seemed near impossible. "But how am I supposed to do that when no true Wizart has been able to come close?" It always seemed like the Wizartry Council gave him impossible tasks. It was like they wanted him to fail.

Riddley leaned forward and placed his hand on Doodles' shoulder. "We are almost certain that the Mayor has his hand in all of this. We just don't know how. You are our inside man at the school. Find out how the Mayor is connected and get the artifact back. Then, I can officially welcome you to the Wizartry world as an elite member amongst our ranks." He beamed like a proud father.

Doodles took a deep breath. Just when he thought there couldn't be any more pressure.

* * *

It was difficult to focus on school work when there was so much going on in his life, but he went through the motions as best he could. In his head, Doodles' thoughts clashed with one another. The field trip had been called off because of the robbery at the museum. Instead, Mrs. Roberts had them painting a plant.

It was a strange feeling to draw with an actual brush and paint when he had gotten so used to drawing with just his hands. It was also rather disappointing to draw something without it coming to life. It was like watering a plant with ketchup knowing full well that the plant wouldn't come to life with that, yet knowing all the while a simple trickle of water would make all the difference.

Doodles kept his eyes on his work but occasionally glanced up at the teacher. He still wasn't sure if she was involved in the Principal's schemes, but he had to find out. She certainly didn't seem like someone that would associate with Mr. Derringer. She was writing some notes and periodically glanced up to smile at the class. After a few more minutes of letting the students paint on their own, she got up and walked around.

Mrs. Roberts was giving advice to one of the students on lighting techniques when the door opened. It was Mr. Derringer. He motioned to Mrs. Roberts. She excused herself and went over to him. No one else seemed to pay any mind, but Doodles was more alert than ever. Mr. Derringer whispered a few things to Mrs. Roberts, too low for Doodles to pick up any of what he was saying, and then handed her a piece of paper. Doodles looked over to Samantha, who gave him a puzzled look, which must have mirrored his own.

She smiled and Mr. Derringer closed the door. Mrs. Roberts headed to her desk and, without reading the paper, she tucked it into her purse.

Doodles was determined to find out what was on that paper. The classroom was too small for him to just get up and walk over there without being noticed. Mrs. Roberts continued to walk around the room giving advice. Her purse was left unattended at the desk. He could run over and snatch it up, but that would be unwise. If only Riddley was here. He was great at creating distractions.

A thought came to Doodles all of a sudden as his thoughts usually did. He began to move his hands, hiding the faint light and movement behind the easel he had been working on. He wasn't sure if this was going to work. Two small mice appeared. He quickly grabbed their tails and picked them up, placing them in the deep pocket of his art smock. He began to walk around the room, as if on his way to the sink, looking casually at the others' works as he went.

When he got to the back of the room by the easel of a girl named Lisa, he casually slipped his hand into his pocket, retrieved the mice, and placed them on her easel when she wasn't looking. Then he quickly went back to his seat.

After a few moments, Lisa screeched and stood up on her stool. The rest of the students began to look around in confusion and worry. Mrs. Roberts hurried over to Lisa's easel.

Doodles took the opportunity to run to the front of the class while everyone was looking at Lisa and trying to figure out what was going on. Then a sudden realization struck. If he took the paper, Mrs. Roberts would know someone had stolen it; instead, he would have to read it quickly and place it back.

Kneeling down, Doodles grabbed the purse and sifted through it to find the paper. He took the paper out and began to read.

*The chief of police is willing to help. Come to my office after all the kids are gone to discuss.*

That's all it said. Willing to help do what? Doodles wondered. But at least he knew now that Mrs. Roberts was in on whatever Mr. Derringer was planning.

"What are you doing?" Mrs. Roberts said.

Doodles looked up. He held his breath. His teacher was standing right next to him, watching him holding her purse open.

As he slowly stood up, he knew he was caught. He literally was holding her purse open. A quick-thinking Doodles blurted out, "I... was looking for some hairspray or something else so we could spray it on the mice and get them to run away out of the classroom," Doodles said. Even as he said it, it sounded ridiculous.

Mrs. Roberts gave him an incredulous look and grabbed her purse. "It isn't acceptable to go through another's personal belongings, Doodles," she said as she looked back at Lisa. "Lisa, is everything okay now?"

Apparently one of the kids had used a broom to goad the mice out of the classroom.

"I am so sorry, Lisa," Mrs. Roberts said. "I will make sure the janitor knows about this." She turned back to Doodles holding up her purse. "And you'd better not let me catch you doing something like this again."

Doodles gulped. Although she turned and smiled at the class, there was a sinister iciness to it this time, an uncanny reminder of Rita.

* * *

Mrs. Roberts made sure that there weren't any lingering students in the hallway. She turned the doorknob and walked into the Principal's office, closing the door behind her.

"So, the police chief is in, just like that?" Mrs. Roberts asked Mr. Derringer who was leaning back in his office chair.

"That's what the note said," he replied, sarcastically.

"I just didn't realize bribing people was so easy," she said. She gave a sneaky smile and Mr. Derringer laughed.

"It's not always so simple," Mr. Derringer replied. "There are many cops that can't be bought. They have an unshakeable moral compass." He chuckled at the thought of people believing in such strict moral codes. "But the chief is really the only person we need for our plan."

"So we are meeting with Rita and Loric tonight to get the fake artifact that Alanso had brought to them, right?" Mrs. Roberts asked.

"Yes," Mr. Derringer replied.

"I just don't understand why we needed the art class or the field trip," she said. "We can't even go on the field trip with the museum closed for investigation. Besides, we already have the real artifact."

He sat up. "The chief told me there is a detective working for him who is very thorough. We got Doodles and his friends into the museum and acting suspiciously around the artifact. By leaving breadcrumbs in the wrong direction, we can ensure that the detective doesn't find out about us. Or at least this gives us time to get away with it."

"Let me guess," Mrs. Roberts said. "The detective is one of those on the force who can't be bribed?"

Mr. Derringer nodded. "We just needed Doodles to think we were up to something. I knew he would search my office because he is full of curiosity and wants to find dirt on me. I left him evidence to make him want to go to the museum. I pulled his strings like a puppeteer." He clapped excitedly. "This is working out better than I could have imagined!"

Mr. Derringer stacked the papers on his desk back into a nice pile. "And now, the chief tells me this detective is hot on Doodles' trail. My plan is all coming together. We'll have access to Inner

Earth whenever we want, and Doodles will be framed. The more he digs into the museum, the more suspicious he looks. I love when stories have happy endings. Let's get going. I'll drive."

\* \* \*

Doodles ducked as low as he could in the seat as Mr. Derringer's car drove by. Uncle Roger held up a map to cover his head. He was simply too large a man to duck while sitting. The Principal's car turned the corner and Uncle Roger threw his own car into reverse and followed. Uncle Roger made sure to stay far enough away that they wouldn't be noticed and close enough so as not to lose sight of Mr. Derringer's car.

Doodles was glad he had called his uncle for help. Not only was Uncle Roger a talented Wizart, but Doodles and his friends were too young to drive. He thought about chasing the car on his bike or drawing something cool like a motorcycle, but someone might get hurt and it just didn't seem worth the risk.

"Do you think they'll notice us?" Darren asked from the back seat. Doodles had nearly forgotten his friends Laura, Samantha, and Darren were in the back seat because they had been so quiet while they waited to follow the Principal.

"I doubt they think anyone is following them," Doodles said.

As they drove, they talked about where they thought Mr. Derringer was heading and focused on staying up with his car. They were so intent on their mission that they were unaware of the undercover police car following them as well.

Sitting in the undercover cruiser, Detective O'Malley smirked. These kids were definitely up to something, O'Malley thought. He hadn't put all the puzzle pieces together, but something big was going on. The kids were following the former Mayor, now turned Principal. Somehow they were all connected. He just had to put the pieces together. In his experience, there were no coincidences.

Uncle Roger's car and the Principal's car stopped in front of a shoe store. The sign on the door read *Closed*, but O'Malley was surprised to see the Principal get out with some lady he didn't recognize and walk right in as if they were expected. Moments later, O'Malley saw Doodles and his friends, along with an accompanying adult, get out of the car and walk into the shop as well.

Detective O'Malley hesitated. Normally, he would call for backup just in case something went wrong, but these were kids and a school principal, and technically, they hadn't done anything wrong. He didn't like using more force than he had to, and he didn't want to scare the kids.

He stopped his car a little further down the street and walked toward the shop. O'Malley sidled up to the front window and peered inside.

The first thing he noticed was the four kids and the adult ducking behind a counter. They peered over the top at the Principal and the woman meeting with the blue-painted giant of a man and the small woman he had seen in the surveillance tape from the museum. Things were getting stranger by the minute. Were these the Wizartry group Doodles had mentioned on the phone? Maybe they were some type of gang. But that didn't sit right with Detective O'Malley. These were too motley of a group to belong together.

O'Malley decided to wait it out and see if anything happened. If he moved too early, he might miss something important. O'Malley crouched down further, watched and waited.

* * *

Doodles leaned towards Uncle Roger and whispered, "I knew he was up to something!"

Uncle Roger nodded. They remained hidden from view as the two groups approached each other.

Alanso suddenly entered through a side door. In his hand he held the artifact.

"Sorry I'm late," Alanso said, grinning.

Rita moaned. "Figured you would be. You never take anything serious," she said.

She then turned to Mr. Derringer and said, "We brought you the artifact like we said we would. In return, we want what you promised," Rita demanded. She grabbed the artifact from Alanso and it held out. Mr. Derringer's eyes lit up and he took a step closer. It was made of gold, a rectangular box with a smaller dome on top made of crystal. The crystal had a slight tinge of rose color embedded in it and sparkled when looked at in certain angles. There were inscriptions, some sort of ancient writing similar to hieroglyphics in the center of the rectangle, which wrapped all the way around the artifact on a bronze plate. On the very top of the dome were three emeralds, cut into diamond shapes, spaced equally apart and glowing with an almost unnatural brilliance. Several feathers lined the artifact, adding to its mysteriousness.

"Hand it to me," he said.

Rita hesitated and then handed it over. "Well, don't just stare at it. Give us what we asked for." Loric took a step forward, and seeing the giant move must have woken Mr. Derringer up from his fascination with the artifact.

He let out a deep and hearty laugh.

"What's so funny?" Rita asked. "I don't have all day to waste with you."

"You'll see," Mr. Derringer said casually. He looked at his watch. "Any moment now."

Rita's eyes widened in surprise. She always had everything planned out and calculated, but in this moment, she knew she had been betrayed. "We have to leave," she said to Loric and Alanso, but it was too late. Dozens of police officers, led by the chief, burst into the store with weapons drawn.

Detective O'Malley followed in after them, confused.

"Freeze!" several of the police officers yelled. Rita, Alanso and Loric reluctantly put their hands up. Against so many they could do nothing. These weren't museum security guards like last time.

The police chief of walked up to them. Doodles could have sworn he saw the chief wink at Mr. Derringer but he wasn't certain. "You're under arrest for the theft of property from Hollyport Museum of Fine Arts. Hands behind your back," the chief said.

"How did you know they were here?" O'Malley asked the chief.

"Not now, O'Malley," the chief replied. Detective O'Malley gave the chief a suspicious look. Something didn't sit right with O'Malley.

"I will get out and I will come after you," Rita whispered to Mr. Derringer.

"Don't forget Doodles. He was the mastermind behind the whole thing," Mr. Derringer said, pointing to the desk that Doodles and his friends Laura, Darren and Samantha and Uncle Roger were hiding behind. Doodles wasn't sure how Mr. Derringer knew they were there, but the policemen came forward and carefully approached Loric and Rita. The policemen took their arms and handcuffed them behind their backs, leading them all away.

"One last thing," the police chief said. "I'll be needing that artifact back from you to return it to its rightful place."

"Of course," Mr. Derringer replied and handed over the artifact.

Mr. Derringer and Mrs. Roberts remained behind as everyone else cleared out. They waited until they were sure everyone was gone. After a few minutes, Mrs. Roberts gave Mr. Derringer an expectant look. He smiled in turn. They shared a knowing look as he reached into his bag. With an even larger smile, he rummaged around in his bag until he pulled out the real artifact.

"And so the puzzle pieces come together. With this artifact, I will have access to Inner Earth whenever I want and Doodles will sit trial for my crime. The irony of it all!"

# Chapter 10

Detective O'Malley of the Hollyport Police Department sat at his desk, reading over an article in the *Hollyport Times*. It just didn't make any sense. Sure, Doodles Lanhorn had clearly been hiding something, but he didn't fit the mold of a hardened criminal, capable of orchestrating a museum heist. He had no prior criminal history and his teachers said he was an attentive and well-mannered student. The article made him out to be some sort of criminal mastermind. Yes, the news tended to exaggerate sometimes, but it just didn't make sense.

The chief insisted that the case was closed and to let it be. Doodles Lanhorn had done the planning and surveillance of the artifact and Loric and Rita were the thieves. Case closed as far as the Hollyport Police Department was concerned. But O'Malley needed the loose ends tied up. He needed to find the rest of the answers. The chief was hiding something, a connection that just wasn't sitting right with O'Malley.

The strange giant named Loric and the woman named Rita were being held in jail until trial. Loric was in restraints to make sure he stayed put. There was a double guard set to watch just him. O'Malley remembered the woman yelling out that walls couldn't stop her. She was clearly a lunatic.

O'Malley kept thinking there were too many holes in this story. How had the chief known where the artifact was, and when to show up at the shoe store meeting? What did Wizartry mean? Was Doodles really the mastermind behind the whole museum heist? How were all these people related? Why was this artifact targeted? Too many questions were running through O'Malley's brain. He needed to get some fresh air and clear his head.

He left the paper on his desk. He had already read the article three times. He wasn't going to get any more answers by staring at it. He left the department and started down the sidewalk. It was a nice, sunny day. O'Malley stopped at the corner cart and grabbed a hot dog with lots of relish and mustard just the way he liked it. He gave the vendor an extra dollar.

Half way through his snack, O'Malley had a thought come to him. He quickly scarfed down the last of the hot dog and tossed the mustard-stained paper into the trash. He walked back to his car and hopped into the driver's seat with his face set in determination. He peeled out into the street. Time to go visit someone.

* * *

Mr. Lanhorn opened the door and after seeing who it was, gave a sour look. "What do you want now?"

Detective O'Malley gave a grin in return. "I know you might not be the police department's biggest fan right now, but I need more answers."

Mr. Lanhorn rolled up his sleeves and crossed his arms. "Haven't you already done enough damage? Now I have to prepare a case to defend my son from ridiculous allegations."

"That's why I'm here," O'Malley said. "Please, if you just let me in to talk to you, I'll explain why I'm here."

The two men stared into each other's eyes, neither backing down. "Fine," Mr. Lanhorn finally said. "I'll give you ten minutes. That's it, and then I want you off my property and to never show your face here again. Understand?"

O'Malley smiled. "Sure thing," he said.

They sat on the living room couch like the last time O'Malley had come here asking questions.

"What, not going to offer me a drink?" O'Malley said, smiling to show he was semi-joking.

Mr. Lanhorn's face turned serious. "Is this a joke to you? This is my son's life we're talking about. You'd better get to the point quick."

O'Malley sighed. "So no drink then. Got it. I'm here because I am good at what I do, Mr. Lanhorn. As much as I think your son is hiding something, and I am sure he is, I strongly believe we have the wrong guy. I just don't see him pulling off a museum heist, especially one of this magnitude."

"You have my attention," Mr. Lanhorn said and then sighed. He realized he was being overly defensive and angry toward someone who was just doing his job.

"There are some strange inconsistencies with the whole thing. If you help me straighten this out, we might be able to build a stronger case for your boy and find the real culprit," O'Malley said.

Doodles' father thought for a minute and then said, "I'll help as long as you continue to search for the truth. My son is innocent."

Detective O'Malley nodded. "He probably is. Then again, maybe I'm wrong. I am a man of hard facts, though, and I plan on getting the whole story. Let's get right to the point. Does Doodles have any enemies?"

Mr. Lanhorn took a minute before he answered, "Yes. Several people over the past year have become very frustrated with Doodles."

"Kids at school?" O'Malley pressed.

"Sure, the kids at his new grade give him a hard time," Doodles' father continued. "But kids have always tried to pick on my son. Kids can be mean like that. But there are several adults who have taken quite a dislike to him too."

"Interesting," O'Malley said. "And who might they be?"

"The former Mayor, who is now principal of my son's school. Also Rita, Alanso and Loric who were also arrested," Mr. Lanhorn said.

"But why would the former Mayor have anything against your son?" O'Malley asked.

"Believe it or not, my son stopped the Mayor from committing a serious crime a few months ago. Doodles was trying to stop him again but he was arrested before he could do so," Mr. Lanhorn said and stood up, pacing back and forth. "My son is a good person. He is honest and has a good heart."

"Do you have any evidence to back up these claims about the Mayor?" Detective O'Malley asked.

Mr. Lanhorn took a deep breath and stopped pacing. "No..."

O'Malley shrugged. "I don't know whether to believe you or not. As I said, I am a man who relies on evidence not hearsay."

"I'm telling you the truth. I'm telling you what I know," Mr. Lanhorn said.

"You might very well be telling me the truth," O'Malley said. "But sometimes not telling the whole truth is as good as lying. Who or what is Wizartry?"

The question took Mr. Lanhorn by surprise. "I..." he fumbled for the proper response.

"I'll stop you right there because I like you," O'Malley said. "I've been doing this detective thing for too many years now and know right away when someone is lying or thinking about lying. Don't bother coming up with a lie. I know just from your reaction that you know who or what Wizartry is. Just tell me so I can help your son!"

Mr. Lanhorn looked to the detective with a calm expression. "I can't tell you what I don't know," he said.

O'Malley stood up as well. "No? So you would rather your son go away to jail for a long time than tell me what or who Wizartry is?"

Mr. Lanhorn pointed towards the door. "I know you're just doing your job, but you've asked enough questions. You can leave now."

Detective O'Malley walked toward the door. "You're making a big mistake withholding information," he said.

"Follow the Mayor instead of asking me more questions," Mr. Lanhorn said as he shut the door as quickly as he could behind the detective.

* * *

Two days later, Doodles sat on the edge of his bed and glumly looked down at the electronic monitor on his ankle. This was no ankle bracelet but at least he was in the comfort of his own home. The monitor wouldn't let him leave the house or else all sorts of alarms would go off. His school work had to be sent to his house for him to work on while he was being kept at home. His mother had seen to that, but he couldn't bring himself to start it. He thought about trying to draw something like a key to get it off, but the risk was too high. He wasn't sure if he tampered with it if the monitor would signal the police and he would be in even more trouble.

Lincoln Middle School had suspended him until after the trial and everything was sorted out. If he was found guilty, he would be expelled. He might have a future with Wizartry, but not if he didn't pass his final test. Being expelled from middle school would be one of the worst things that could happen to him. He would be hard-pressed to get into college and find a decent job, and without being a full Wizart, he would not have any opportunity there either. He would be in the same boat Brandon was in and that was a horrible thought. Even though Brandon was a bully who had tormented Doodles for many years, he felt bad for the kid going down a road that would only lead to a more difficult life. He didn't want that for himself.

His friends and Uncle Roger were also wearing electronic monitoring devices and were confined to their own homes. The police said that it was to ensure they didn't run off or hide prior to getting all the information out of them and to reach a decision on what was to happen to them.

Doodles stayed in contact with them through text messages and over the phone, but it wasn't the same. They were equally as upset as he was and concerned for their futures as well they should be. They couldn't talk freely because Doodles' father had warned them that their phones might now be bugged in an effort to catch them saying something incriminating. Uncle Roger assured him this would all work itself out, but Doodles wasn't so sure.

This is all my fault, Doodles thought. He slumped his head into his hands and moaned. If he hadn't brought his friends into this, they wouldn't be in trouble. He got them involved in this situation. Doodles shook his head to clear it. No, Doodles thought, starting to feel more hopeful, they were his friends and they were there for him just like he was there for them. They would all find a way to get through this.

Doodles began to pace his room, thinking of ways to get out of this situation. What if... He grabbed the phone and began to dial.

"Detective O'Malley, please," Doodles said into the phone.

"Who is speaking?" a gruff voice from the other end asked.

"Tell him Doodles Lanhorn wants to speak to him," Doodles said and then he lowered his voice, realizing that if his father heard him from down the hall, he would be quite upset for contacting the detective without first consulting him.

There was a minute or so of quiet from the other end of the phone and then O'Malley picked up.

"This is Detective O'Malley."

"Hi. It's me, Doodles Lanhorn," Doodles said.

"What's going on, kid?"

"I just thought of something. My Dad said you came here because you aren't done with the case and that you were looking for evidence. If you really want to find out what happened, check the Principal's office at my school. There is a book there that has all the museum guard schedules and information in the Mayor's handwriting. It clearly shows he was planning the museum heist," Doodles explained. "Don't you think it makes more sense that an adult with motives and means came up with a plan to steal an artifact and not some thirteen-year-old kid?"

"Why didn't you bring this up before?" O'Malley asked.

"I didn't think of it until just now and I also didn't know if I could trust you," Doodles said. "Also, I don't really have any choice now. I'm scared and innocent."

"What makes you trust me now?" O'Malley asked.

"Because you want to find out the truth," Doodles said. He looked down at his ankle bracelet in frustration. "Please, just look. It's the Principal you want to focus on. Trust me."

There was a pause.

"I'll look into it but I'm not making any promises. The chief said the case is closed, so getting a warrant might prove difficult."

"Thank you for at least taking a look," Doodles said.

Doodles was about to hang up when O'Malley said, "Hey kid."

"Yes?" Doodles asked.

"Sit tight and in the meantime, don't do anything foolish," Detective O'Malley said.

* * *

Doodles was growing impatient. He had been stuck in his house for two days straight. The preliminary hearing was tomorrow to decide if there was enough evidence to go to trial. His life would be completely ruined. Unfortunately the warrant to search Mr. Derringer's office had been denied.

He knew that Detective O'Malley had told him not to do anything, but he never said anything about involving Boogley.

"I know that look," Boogley said from inside of Doodles' closet door. Boogley had been sifting through Doodles' pile of dirty laundry looking for shoes. Doodles had caught Boogley quite a few times nibbling on his shoelaces, a habit that Doodles no longer found cute.

"What look?" Doodles asked.

"You have an idea in your head. Luckily I am always up for an adventure," Boogley said as he puffed his chest out with pride.

Doodles smiled at his small, furry friend. "With me stuck in the house and the warrant denied, there is no way to prove my innocence without getting that book to Detective O'Malley. I need you to get in there somehow and get me that book."

Boogley hopped up and down in excitement. "I'm on it!"

He scurried toward the door on his webbed feet until Doodles called out and he screeched to a halt.

"Wait! Grab some of his other papers so that they can match up his handwriting," Doodles added.

"Great idea!" Boogley said.

He hurried off. Doodles was left in his room by himself. This was his last hope. He trusted Boogley, but so many things could go wrong with this plan. Doodles began to draw with his hands, shimmering light following his every move. With a popping sound, a tennis ball appeared. He lay down on his bed and began to toss the ball up into the air. One day would decide his fate. One day would decide if he would continue and go on to high school, be able to pass his Wizartry test, or if he would have a criminal record and maybe even go to a juvenile detention center.

# Chapter 11

Boogley fell through an open window and landed on his side. He jumped up and looked left. He looked right. He looked up at the ceiling just in case. He was taking this secret agent mission very seriously. This was no joking matter. He had to get that book. Doodles had done so much for him. In fact, he wouldn't even exist if it weren't for Doodles.

The hallway sure looked empty. Boogley looked back and forth a few more times just to be certain. Luckily, if someone was around, Boogley's steps were muffled by his fur so that he could be as quiet as a mouse.

He darted down the hallway and ducked into the first alcove. He peered around the wall and took another look down the hallway. No one in sight. *Unless that's what they want me to think*, Boogley thought. He rushed to the next doorway and then the next. It took a few minutes, but he made it to the Principal's office.

The door was locked, but that never stopped Boogley before. He opened his mouth to reveal a set of extremely long, pointed teeth. Obviously they would know someone had broken in, but by that time, hopefully the Principal would be behind bars.

Boogley began to chew on the door. It tasted terrible! Not nearly as delicious as Doodles' shoelaces. He chewed and gnawed in Boogley-like fashion and before long there was a good sized hole in the door. He poked his head inside.

Seeing nobody, Boogley hopped through the hole he had made and scrambled into the room. The lights were off and Boogley didn't have great vision in the dark. He was too short to reach the light switch and so he wound up bumping into almost every piece of furniture in the room. Maybe the book was gone. Maybe he wouldn't find it and let Doodles down.

It took several minutes before he finally found the book on the desk but under a big pile of papers. His short stubby hands were not good for gripping so he had to carefully pick up the papers and book with his teeth and put the book into a bag he found in the waste basket. Boogley then grabbed the bag with his teeth and headed out. No wasting time. That's how people get caught. *I'm coming, Doodles!*

Boogley ran down the hallway and out the window he had snuck into to get into the school. Now all he had to do was make it back home safely.

* * *

Doodles paced nervously back and forth across his bedroom floor. The police ankle bracelet was starting to irritate his skin. He had an itch that he just couldn't seem to reach no matter what he did or used. He had even tried getting at the itch by twisting a clothes hanger that he could push but it just didn't seem to make it feel any better.

The hearing was scheduled for the next morning and Boogley still wasn't back yet. He was taking way longer than he should have taken.

His door swung open suddenly just as he was about to finally reach the spot on his ankle that itched so very badly. He thought Boogley would come waddling inside. He didn't expect Detective O'Malley and his parents to walk in.

His father gave Doodles a stern look. "I don't appreciate being lied to," he said.

Doodles said, "I didn't lie. I just didn't say anything."

"I don't want to hear it. Just keep me in the loop next time," Mr. Lanhorn said. "We love you but when you act like this, it makes your mother and I worry."

Mrs. Lanhorn wrapped her arm around her husband.

Detective O'Malley cleared his throat. All eyes turned to him. "I now fully believe your story, as crazy as it sounded before," he said. "My instincts and the evidence now points toward the Mayor. But..." He made sure to look at each person's face.

"There are still two major issues," O'Malley said. "First off, I still think Doodles is hiding something about this Wizartry thing or person. That irritates me. You should listen to your father and be more open and honest. Secondly, and much more pressing at the moment, is that this evidence that magically appeared on my doorstep, as damning as it is against the Mayor, may not be admissible in court."

"What?" Doodles yelled out louder than he intended.

"I can't admit that the evidence was on my doorstep," O'Malley explained. "It sounds too unbelievable. And I can't and won't lie about it. That's not who I am. The police chief told me not to investigate and I was denied a warrant. If anything, I will be suspended and investigated for disobeying a direct order and seizure of property without proper warrants. You actually put my career in jeopardy!"

"I never intended for that to happen!" Doodles explained. "Please, isn't there a way?"

Detective O'Malley turned toward his father. "Isn't he the lawyer? Ask him."

Doodles looked to his father, who said, "You should have asked me first. We could have tried to do this the right way."

"But if we did, then the Principal would have found out about it and hid the evidence," Doodles said. "Then we wouldn't have any case against him."

"There might be one route we can take. It might be risky, but it may be the only way," Mr. Lanhorn said.

Detective O'Malley eyed him somewhat suspiciously. "A legal way, right?"

"I'll admit it's a bit of a grey area, but nothing extreme," Mr. Lanhorn said. "We take the evidence and our story and we bring it to a news reporter. If they run the story, which with the evidence and the scope of the news, they should, then with all of the public knowing, charges may be dropped.

"And you won't be implicated," Mr. Lanhorn added, "because news reporters always protect their sources."

Detective O'Malley thought about it for a few seconds and then said, "I'll allow that. I am always a strong believer in freedom of the press. But I can't be a part of it. You will have to go on your own."

Doodles and his parents nodded.

"You'll have to stay here with your ankle bracelet, sweetie," his mother said. "Try to rest up for tomorrow." She gave Doodles a kiss on the top of his head. "We'll be back as soon as we can. If you get hungry, there are leftovers in the fridge. Just heat them up."

Doodles gave her a smile and pretended that he wasn't afraid of their plan not working out, which would leave him with the imminent trial.

\* \* \*

Doodles waited again. He couldn't sleep, he couldn't rest, and his ankle was itching again with renewed fury. All of this waiting made him feel like the world was passing him by and he could only observe through a glass cage. Things were out of his control. He had to trust that everything would work out, but it was just so tough on him. The only good outcome was that Rita, Alanso and Loric were in prison. However, without the authorities knowing about Wizartry, it seemed unlikely that they could hold them for long. Rita was the most devious person he had ever met and that, coupled with her irrational urge to seek revenge on the Wizartry Council, meant she was still dangerous.

If his parents were successful, the news station would break the story and the city would have no choice but to investigate and file charges against Mr. Derringer. His own charges would be dropped, and he could move on with his life in middle school and his final Wizartry test. He would have access to Inner Earth whenever he wanted! If only he could hold onto that wonderful dream. With everything happening in his current situation, though, the dream felt like an elusive, far away mirage and he was sinking slowly into a pit of quicksand. Doodles' vivid imagination began to paint a clearer and clearer picture of him trying to hold his head above the sand, gasping for his last breaths.

Doodles shook his head to clear it. It had almost felt like a panic attack. Wasn't he too young to have one of those?

He picked up one of his favorite books, *Harry Potter and the Sorcerer's Stone*, and began to read. He had to keep his mind off of what was going on no matter how daunting a task that seemed. There were too many things that could go wrong. The news station could be closed by now. They could reject airing any of it. There... Doodles threw his book across his room in frustration. It slammed against the far wall. Doodles wanted desperately to come up with some creative solution to his problems, but he couldn't even leave his own house!

He forced himself to take a few deep breaths. He closed his eyes and breathed, listening for his own breath going in and out. He had to pull it together.

The phone rang. He opened his eyes and walked over to his phone he had left on the nightstand next to his bed. He didn't feel like talking to anyone, but it could be important.

"Hello?" Darren asked from the other end.

"Hey, Darren," Doodles replied, trying his best to sound cheerful. He didn't want his friend to get discouraged.

"How are you holding up?" Darren asked.

"As best I can. But it will all work out," Doodles said, trying to convince himself as much as to convince Darren. "My parents are bringing my book, the one the Principal stole, to the news station. If it works out, our charges could be dropped."

"That's great news!" Darren said.

"We're not out of this yet," Doodles warned. "I'll let you guys know as soon as I hear back. Is it okay if I call your house late tonight?"

"Of course!" Darren exclaimed.

"Good. I'll let you know what happens," Doodles said. He hung up before Darren asked more questions.

* * *

"Doodles! We're home!" His Mom's voice called from downstairs. It was the greatest sound in the world to hear his mother's voice again. It had seemed like an eternity since they had left, every minute a painstaking reminder of the situation he was in.

"Come see this!" his father called out.

Doodles ran out of his room and down the stairs. He found his parents in his living room. They were standing and looking at the television.

He looked at the television and his mouth opened in surprise. The Principal's face was in the corner of the screen. Along the bottom, a headline read, "School Principal scandal leads to arrest of art thief."

A woman reporter stood in front of Mr. Derringer's house. Doodles recognized her from the local station. Doodles' father turned the volume up. They listened intently as the reporter said, "Moments ago, the Principal of Lincoln Middle School and former Mayor, Shane Derringer, was arrested by the F.B.I. based on new evidence that has turned up in the Hollyport Fine Arts Museum case. It looks like there is a clear trail of evidence leading back to Mr. Derringer. The F.B.I., in a surprise move, has also taken the Hollyport Police Chief into custody after allegations surfaced of bribery and cover up. Apparently, the F.B.I. has been following Derringer's movements on the grounds of suspected tax evasion and several unsubstantiated reports of bribery. More on this story coming up next."

Mr. Lanhorn turned the television off and smiled.

Doodles cheered and hugged his parents. "You did it!" he yelled to them.

His father smiled. "No, *we* did it." Doodles savored this moment and tried to burn it into his memory so he would never forget this happy turnout. He kept his parents in an embrace and thought about how much he loved his family.

# CHAPTER 12

Detective O'Malley knelt down and removed the ankle bracelet from Doodles' ankle.

"Bet you're happy to get this off," O'Malley said.

The first thing Doodles did when it was fully removed was scratch his ankle. It felt so good to have it taken off, not only physically, but symbolically as well. He was free.

"More than you know," Doodles replied.

"Now remember," Detective O'Malley said. "Stay out of trouble," he continued as he smiled.

When the detective left, Doodles' uncle entered the room. "Looks like you'll be able to make your final test after all!" Uncle Roger said as he made his way across the room to Doodles. "My car's out front. Are you ready?"

Everything had happened so quickly. Doodles felt kind of guilty that he had thought about the trial as an excuse to not have to take the final test. It wasn't that he didn't want to become a full Wizart. It was just that he was afraid of failing.

"I'm ready," Doodles told his uncle.

"I am so proud of you, no matter how it goes at your final test today!" Uncle Roger exclaimed. He gave a hearty laugh and clapped Doodles on the back.

"Can you give me any advice?" Doodles asked his uncle.

"You have many skills and strengths, Doodles. All of them will prove useful, but your creativity is what will be needed here. Don't let the spectators or the Council distract you. Clear your mind and open it to your creative side. That's all I can really tell you. It's the Final Wizartry test, after all."

Doodles tried to smile and nodded.

"Well then, let's get going!" Uncle Roger said. "Not the best idea to keep the Wizartry Council waiting."

Doodles followed his uncle downstairs and out to the curb where his uncle's car was waiting. They got in and drove off. Neither Doodles nor his uncle noticed Detective O'Malley's car pull out and follow them.

Detective O'Malley kept well back but close enough that he didn't lose sight of the vehicle. Where was Doodles off to in such a hurry? He had been cooped up in the house for a few days. The kid was probably asking for a ride to grab fast food. But he had a feeling there was more going on. The kid wasn't the museum thief, but he was certainly hiding something important. Of that much he was certain.

He followed Uncle Roger's car for several streets. The car then pulled up along the curb in front of a small flower shop. Why would the first place the kid goes to be a flower shop?

Detective O'Malley made sure to drive past and park in front of a hardware store a few doors down. Luckily there were plenty of other cars parked along the road so that his car didn't stand out. Doodles Lanhorn was a mystery, and O'Malley didn't like to leave anything fully unsolved.

O'Malley watched as Doodles and his uncle went into the flower shop. Detective O'Malley decided it would be best to wait outside. He could always go in afterward and ask questions. The shop was so small that if he walked in he would be spotted right away. O'Malley chuckled out loud at the thought of explaining why he was also in the same small flower shop.

Time went by and no one came outside. A few people went in but no one came out in over twenty minutes. O'Malley grew suspicious. It would be pretty tightly packed in there by now. He tapped the steering wheel anxiously. What was going on in there? What was so special about some small flower shop on Lamter Lane?

* * *

Doodles Lanhorn found himself standing in front of the Wizartry Council once again. You would think that by now Doodles would feel more comfortable, but all three were intimidating in their long black robes and ornate Wizartry hats. Doodles knew his uncle and Riddley were in attendance in the spectator stands, but it was so dark up there that he couldn't recognize any one.

As was customary, Charles, the eldest of the Council members, spoke first.

"This is a big day for you, Doodles Lanhorn," Charles said. "Your past exploits, especially saving me and Inner Earth, are brave deeds indeed. However much we want you to join our ranks, it is Wizartry tradition that you pass the final test."

Council Member Brian laughed. "The final test will not be so easy. Although my fellow Council members think very highly of you, I think you have just been lucky so far. Do not worry. If you fail this test, and I think there is a decent chance that you will, you can retake it in six months when your skills have improved."

Doodles didn't understand why Brian hated him so much. He hadn't done anything to offend the man that he knew of. In fact, Doodles had helped the Wizartry Council many times. The man should be grateful.

"Why do you hate me so much?" Doodles asked before he could think better of it. The crowd grew completely silent as the faint murmuring of whispered conversations suddenly ceased.

"Excuse me?" Brian asked. "I never said I hated you."

Doodles thought Brian looked mean before, but now his eyes narrowed and his lips grew into a snarl. "The only thing I hate is that you don't use your full potential. I've said enough. Let's get on with the test already."

Council Member Holly held up a calming hand. "Yes, let us proceed."

This was it. This one test would decide if he was to become a full Wizart. Being a full Wizart would mean that he would have unlimited access to Inner Earth, gain respect from fellow Wizarts, and learn about all the secrets and history of Wizartry. Doodles wanted this more than anything else in his life. This was the moment he had been training so hard for.

"Doodles, are you paying attention?" Brian asked. "See, this is why I get annoyed. You have a faraway look in your eyes as if you are daydreaming about something else. How are we to take you seriously if you don't take this test seriously?"

Doodles swallowed nervously and stood up straight. "I assure you that I do take this very seriously. I'm just a little nervous."

Brian shook his head. "We will see. Prove yourself."

Charles stood up and cleared his throat. "Well, Doodles. It is time." He grabbed his paint brush and painted a flaming torch. With it, Charles held it up to a row of lanterns packed neatly together along the wall. With a loud swoosh, the fire took off, and all the lanterns were lit almost instantaneously, illuminating the entire room.

Doodles noted that there were far more spectators present today than for his last test. There were many people he did not recognize. In fact, all of the seats were filled. Some people even stood in the back watching with excitement clearly visible on their faces, standing on tip toes to get a better view. Talk about pressure!

Charles pulled an ornately-carved wooden box from underneath a table and held it out toward Doodles. It had blue lettering along its exterior, similar to the tattoos Doodles had seen on Loric. They glowed with a faint blue light.

"When I open this box, your test begins," Charles said.

* * *

Doodles took a ready stance. He didn't know what to expect. His hands were at his sides like the gunslingers in the old western television show his father used to watch.

The box opened and a blinding, brilliant yellow light shot out in all directions. Doodles covered his eyes against the glare. He couldn't see. Every time he tried to peek through the gaps in his fingers, his eyes burned from the light.

As suddenly as the light came, it vanished. Doodles opened his eyes, expecting to see some sort of angry and powerful creature before him.

It wasn't a creature. It wasn't a stranger. It was someone he knew too well. It was himself, Doodles. Only, it couldn't be real. It had to be some sort of mirage. The Doodles he saw before him looked somewhat younger.

Charles spoke as the two Doodles stared at each other. "The final test has always been the same for centuries. This is your chance to prove that you have grown in power and creativity and overall Wizartry skill. You must best yourself from a few months ago. The hardest enemy is sometimes yourself."

The younger Doodles began to paint with his hands. He was quick and he was confident in his skill.

Doodles began to paint too. He had grown a lot in the last few months. He wouldn't let his younger self stop him from becoming a Wizart.

They both finished at about the same time. Doodles didn't have the luxury of time to wonder how it was possible that another Doodles was standing in front of him. Wizartry was full of surprises, dating back centuries. Whenever Doodles thought he knew everything, a new skill or artifact was revealed. He had to concentrate on this moment, and this moment alone.

Since neither the current Doodles nor the younger version of Doodles knew what the other was painting, it would be left up to chance. But that wasn't necessarily true. In the quick seconds each had to decide what to paint, they both had imagined what the other would fear the most.

The spectators gasped and the Wizartry Council stood up from their seats in amusement and excitement. The younger Doodles had thought of what scared him the most, while Doodles had thought of what would scare the younger version of him in order to win the challenge and pass his test. The result, although derived from different reasoning, was that they painted the same exact thing.

Two copies of Ricky, the school bully, stood facing each other. Each Doodles squirmed nervously, taking a few steps back. The two Rickys approached each other, ready to show the other who was the stronger. Doodles realized with a start that he was acting just like his younger self. If he was acting just as afraid as he was months ago, then how would that show he had grown at all? Doodles was so tired of being afraid, of being bullied or left out of activities at school, of being made fun of for being different, and most importantly, he was sick of having to constantly remind himself that he wasn't a loser like his peers called him.

His face flushed with anger. The spectators, the Rickys, the Wizartry Council all faded into a hazy background. His vision began to blur, his hands trembling. It felt like he had to release his anger, like a powerful current was building up inside of him with nowhere to go. His whole body began to ache, his anger growing steadily instead of subsiding. With a gasp, he held up a trembling hand and pointed it at the Rickys and the younger Doodles.

The spectators were shouting but Doodles could not hear any of it. The only sound he heard was his heartbeat and the energy flowing through his body.

Bright swirls of color shot from his outstretched hand and like tentacles the streams of color wrapped around the Wizartry creations of the Rickys and the younger Doodles. The colors wrapped tighter and tighter until the colors completely covered their bodies. With a last tremble of his hand, Doodles watched in fascination as the hazy images before him disappeared. His hearing started to return. His heartbeat slowed. Sweat dripped from his forehead. The swirls of color dissipated.

Doodles dropped to the floor in exhaustion and passed out.

* * *

From behind a support beam, Detective O'Malley watched the scene unfold. It had been rather easy to sneak past the guy guarding the entrance. He couldn't believe what he was seeing. This had to be "Wizartry". This was some type of magic. Everything he had ever believed in, logic, hard work, rules were all swept out from beneath him. The very foundation of who he was and the way he thought the world worked was gone in an instant.

O'Malley watched as several people ran over to help Doodles. He was sitting up now in a daze. O'Malley was too far away to hear what was being said, but with all the confusion, he realized he should take this opportunity to sneak out.

Doodles tried to talk but his throat was too hoarse. It was almost like he had been screaming at the top of his lungs for a long time. He was exhausted. He looked around. People gathered around him, some with concern, others with confusion or even fear.

He tried to remember what had happened, but it all felt like a dream.

"Did... Did I pass the test?" Doodles finally managed to ask.

Council Member Brian looked down at him. His stern look softened and he smiled.

"Welcome to the Wizarts." Brian placed a hat onto Doodles' head. It was made out of fine material and fit perfectly. It was dark green with a light green rim. Beads of all different colors also lined the rim.

"I... What happened?" Doodles asked.

Council Member Holly helped him up with a tug of his hand and steadied him. Doodles felt weak and woozy. "You never cease to amaze us, Doodles Lanhorn. First you learned to perform Wizartry without use of a paint brush, an advanced skill only the ancient Wizarts knew how to employ. Then you did something no one has any record of a Wizart being able to do. You were able to erase multiple drawings without use of dissolving ink. These abilities make you a very rare commodity."

"I don't know how I did that, and I don't know if I can do it again," Doodles admitted. "In fact, I think I may have overexerted myself."

Brian spoke up and said, "Yes, but if you can learn to control that ability, you could be a very powerful Wizart and a great asset to the Wizartry Council."

Doodles' head was finally starting to clear. "So I have unlimited access to Inner Earth now?"

Holly laughed and said, "Yes. We will register your name with the gatekeeper at the flower shop. You can come and go as you please."

Doodles' eyes lit up at the freedom he now had. He had wanted this for so long now and it came as sort of a shock. It was all too sudden. "So what now?" Doodles asked.

"Wear the hat with pride," Council Member Charles said. "No one can see a Wizart hat but other Wizarts and those that are friends of Wizarts. It takes someone who is keen on colors and light to recognize another Wizart."

The three Wizartry Council members looked at each other and nodded. Charles said, "You meet with the Wizartry Emperor tomorrow. He will want to talk to you."

"Wizartry Emperor?" Doodles asked. "I thought that the Wizartry Council members were the leaders."

Charles explained, "We enforce the laws, but the Emperor makes them."

"Who is he and how come no one ever told me about him?" Doodles asked.

The crowd of spectators had cleared the room. Doodles was left alone with the three members of the Wizartry Council.

Charles responded, "You will find out much more in the days to come. Wizartry tries to keep things hidden until a member officially joins our ranks. It serves many purposes, but mainly it is for security reasons."

He took out a few pieces of paper from his robe pocket. Charles continued, "The Council has a lot of business to attend to today. Come here tomorrow to meet with us and the Emperor. All your questions will be answered then."

Doodles wanted to ask more questions, but the Wizartry Council had already begun to discuss business matters, a clear sign that it was his time to leave.

He looked around and then left. Doodles wore his new Wizartry hat with pride. He had passed his final test. He was a Wizart.

Uncle Roger waited outside in front of his car. "I knew you could do it!" he said, a huge grin spreading from ear to ear on his face. "Welcome to the Wizarts!"

Doodles flashed a smile in return and tipped his Wizartry hat. Uncle Roger chuckled. "You have to tell me more about what you did in there. I've never seen anyone draw with just their hands and be able to erase drawings without dissolving ink!"

He shrugged as they seated themselves in the car. "Don't really understand it either," he said.

Uncle Roger said, "Well, we'll have time to figure that out later. For now, let's get you home to celebrate."

"Uncle Roger?"

"Yes?"

"How come no one ever told me about the Wizartry Emperor?" Doodles asked.

Uncle Roger kept his eyes focused on the road. "The Emperor is a very secretive man," Roger began. He put his left turn signal on as they stopped at a red light a few blocks from home. "He sticks to tradition, and our tradition has always been to reveal certain inner workings of Wizartry only after people become full Wizartry members. Knowledge of all our workings is earned as a new Wizart grows and proves himself or herself to be trustworthy."

Doodles nodded and sat quietly with his thoughts for the rest of the ride home. Uncle Roger was driving very slowly to give Doodles time to feel more settled, but Doodles didn't mind. He was excited that he had passed the final test and had the opportunity to meet the Emperor, but he was also nervous about what had happened back in the test area. He had become so angry that he had lost control of his body and actions. It was a scary thought.

The car finally pulled into the driveway of Doodles' house. Uncle Roger turned the car off and opened his door, stepping out. Doodles followed. They walked up the long driveway and onto the stone steps leading up to his house.

Something wasn't right. The front door was open a crack and his parents never left the door unlocked. Doodles readied himself. Maybe Rita or Loric had escaped prison and had come for revenge. After everything he had been through, Doodles figured that he had the right to be cautious.

Uncle Roger didn't seem to think anything was amiss. He opened the door for Doodles, who walked through slow and prepared.

As soon as Doodles walked inside, he was met by many loud shouts.

\* \* \*

"Surprise!" everyone yelled. Doodles felt like he had almost had a heart attack. His hands had been squeezed so tight in anticipation of something wrong that they had turned nearly purple.

His mother and father were sitting on the living room couch. Aunt Martha was there as well as many other Wizartry members. His best friends, Darren, Laura and Samantha, who were

93

by now trusted by the Wizartry community to keep secret, were there as well.

Riddley was standing in the corner with a soda in his hand. He sniffed it and put it down. "Terribly poisonous stuff," he said. "Oh, and congratulations are in order. Must have had a good trainer!" The room laughed at Riddley's quip.

Doodles could not remember a time when he had been happier or prouder of himself. He really had come a long way in a very short amount of time.

"Look at your hat!" Laura exclaimed as she came up to him. "I'm kind of jealous," she said and smiled. "Even though I am proud of you, I still think that hat would look better on me," she teased.

"Will you take us back into Inner Earth again?" Darren asked.

"I wish I could," Doodles said. "Last time was an exception. Inner Earth is only for Wizarts," he said and winked at them as he moved on to greet everyone else. They laughed.

"Proud of you," Samantha said. Doodles was thankful she hadn't brought up ditching his friends again. Maybe she was okay with them now.

Aunt Martha greeted him with a big hug and an embarrassingly long kiss on his cheek. Doodles was sure that he must have lipstick left on him. He casually wiped at his cheek with his sleeve.

After saying hello and thanking the rest of the Wizarts for coming, Doodles finally made his way to his parents by the couch at the far end of the living room.

"Took you long enough," his father started. "Thought you were busy signing autographs for your fans," he joked.

Doodles laughed in turn. "No, just saying hello."

His mother gave him a big hug. "Don't forget where you come from and where home will always be." She let go of her embrace and kept her hands on both of his shoulders, looking into his eyes with pride. "Don't forget us old folks, okay?"

"Of course not," Doodles said. "I love you guys."

His father's face turned somewhat more serious. "Don't want to put a damper on your party, but even though you are a full Wizart, you are too young to go adventuring through Inner Earth whenever you want. We are still your parents and you are still a kid and we need to know when you are going."

"I promise I will communicate with you," Doodles assured them.

"Good," his father said. "That's all I want. Now go hang out with your friends. I hear you have a big day tomorrow." He winked and Doodles smiled and turned to go find Darren and Laura again.

All of a sudden, just when things seemed to be quieting down, the doorbell rang. The room silenced. Doodles froze. He was still shaking inside, a result of all that had happened during his third test.

Uncle Roger turned toward Mr. Lanhorn. "You expecting anyone else?" Uncle Roger asked.

Doodles' father shook his head. "No," he responded. "Everyone act normal. I'll go see who it is." The room remained silent as Mr. Lanhorn walked across the living room and put his hand on the doorknob. He turned it slowly and pulled it open.

In the doorway stood Detective O'Malley of the Hollyport Police Department. "Can I come in?" he asked.

Mr. Lanhorn eyed the detective suspiciously but opened the door. "We are in the middle of a small party. Can you come back later?"

"I'll be quick, Mr. Lanhorn, I promise," O'Malley said.

"Fine, but please try to make it quick," Mr. Lanhorn said.

O'Malley stepped inside and closed the front door behind him. All eyes were on him.

"In all my years of service, I have never felt this out of place. The world is not what I thought it was," O'Malley addressed the entire room. "I know who you all are, but I don't understand how or why you can do what you do." The Wizarts looked at each other uncertainly. This was not something that happened often. Wizartry was supposed to be a well-kept secret.

"Sit down," Uncle Roger said in a loud and commanding voice.

O'Malley looked around him at the men and women and then sat on a chair by the couch.

"We have a lot to talk about," Uncle Roger said carefully.

"I need some answers," O'Malley said. "I want to know everything about Wizartry and I want to know it now. As an officer of the law I have to be able to protect the people of Hollyport from any perceived threat. And right now I do not know if you all are a threat or not."

Uncle Roger gave the detective a skeptical look and then looked at Doodles. "Can this man be trusted?"

"Yes. He acts tough but he's really a nice guy. He is one of the good cops. He's the one that helped me prove my innocence," Doodles said.

O'Malley added. "I think I already know what you all can do. I just want to understand it."

Uncle Roger took a deep breath and took a chair next to the detective. "What I am about to tell you remains in this room, understood?"

O'Malley nodded. "Yes," he said. "I would sound crazy telling people anyways. Wouldn't want to lose my job or be forced to see a shrink, would I? The only reason I believe it is because I saw this Wizartry with my own eyes."

"Very well," Uncle Roger said. "I'll start with the basics."

# Chapter 13

Over the course of the next few hours, several Wizarts helped piece together the information on Wizartry they felt was safe to divulge. Detective O'Malley shook his head. "I can't believe all of this," he said. "It's amazing..."

"Well, that's our story. Now you know everything we can tell you and you can put your curiosity to rest," Uncle Roger said.

"It's not so simple," O'Malley said.

Doodles noticed that his uncle's hand was close to the paint brush at his side. Doodles hoped this didn't end badly. He didn't want his uncle to get into trouble with the law if he tried something using Wizartry.

"What do you mean?" Uncle Roger asked. "We told you what you wanted. Not to be rude, but isn't it time for you to go?"

"I want to ask Mr. and Mrs. Lanhorn something before I leave," O'Malley said. "I promise I'll leave as soon as you answer, and regardless of the response, you have my word I will keep quiet about this. Besides, like I said, no one would believe me anyways."

Mr. Lanhorn gave a smile. "We have come to trust you, Detective. What do you want to ask?"

O'Malley thought about how to phrase his question and then looked at Doodles. "The new police chief is changing things up.

He is making me the head of a special task force, assigned to investigate intricate cases like the museum heist. I would like to ask if Doodles could assist me in some of the investigations. I assure you he would never be in harm's way, and with his help and my skills, we could really make a difference around here."

All eyes looked at Doodles and then to Mr. Lanhorn as he said, "Only investigating, right?"

Detective O'Malley nodded and said, "Yes. I give you my word. I would never put a kid in harm's way. When I saw what Wizartry can do, I knew right away it could be put to good use."

Mr. Lanhorn thought about it for a few seconds. "If Doodles' skill can help make a difference in Hollyport, then yes. But it can't put him in harm's way and it can't interfere with his school work."

O'Malley chuckled. "It won't. It's like when some of our detectives get desperate and contact a local psychic or something for leads, only in this case, of course, Doodles' powers are real."

Detective O'Malley hung around for a few more minutes and then left. Most of the Wizarts were happy when the detective left. During his visit, it had made the party goers quiet and left them feeling awkward. Doodles' friends thought it was so neat that he was going to be working for the police department, but Doodles wasn't sure if he wanted to, yet. He felt like he might be taking on too many tasks at the same time. He had to learn that he couldn't say yes to everything. A lot of his current teachers advised the students that when they reached high school, they would have to learn how to prioritize or else they might become overwhelmed and do a poor job.

He tried to enjoy the rest of the party, but now all he could think about was meeting the Emperor tomorrow and about working for the police department. Detective O'Malley could now call on Doodles to investigate some of his toughest cases whenever he needed him. This was all very exciting, but it brought a lot of anxiety with it. There was always something to worry about in his life.

Doodles saw Samantha talking to his friends. He came over just in time to hear Samantha say, "I owe you two an apology. I didn't realize how good you are for Doodles. You really are good friends."

Laura smiled. "Thanks."

"I'm just happy you guys let me into your lives. I've never had so much excitement and fun," Samantha said.

Doodles smiled. They were finally getting along.

* * *

Uncle Roger dropped Doodles off in front of the flower shop. Doodles wore his new Wizart's hat and he had his backpack with him.

"Good luck today," Uncle Roger said. "I remember my first time meeting the Emperor. He was much younger then. He was a great man then and still is. He organized the Wizartry world and led them with confidence at just twenty years of age. He established rules and laws that keep the Wizartry world safe from prying eyes and those who would seek to destroy or abuse its powers."

"I look forward to meeting him," Doodles said. He gave his uncle a nod and then entered the shop. He waved hello to the gatekeeper and entered the stairwell leading down to the Wizartry Council chamber.

There, he was met by the three Council members. They stood waiting for him. Behind him, sitting on a chair was an old man.

"Welcome back, Doodles," Council Member Holly said. "We are very proud to have you as a member of the Wizarts. Maybe one day you will think about running for the Council. That is, if Charles ever decides to retire." She gave Council Member Charles a sly grin and he in turn laughed.

"I'll retire when I am well ready to," Charles said. "Besides, I already have my land and house picked out in Inner Earth. They aren't going anywhere."

Council Member Brian pointed toward the elderly man behind them. "That is our Emperor. He governs over all Wizartry affairs. The Wizartry Council is his judicial branch while he is the executive. We have kept him up to speed on your progress. He is very interested in meeting you."

The Wizartry Council members waved Doodles forward. He took a few hesitant steps. He really didn't have anything to be afraid of. He had already passed his test and was now a full Wizartry member. So why did he have butterflies in his stomach? Why did his knees feel wobbly?

As Doodles slowly approached, he removed his hat and studied the man before him. He didn't look like anything spectacular, at least not enough so to garner a name like Emperor, in Doodles' opinion, but then he wasn't exactly sure what an Emperor should look like. Then again, Doodles had learned the hard way that looks can be deceiving, like Rita and her tiny, innocent look when he had run into her on his first trip to Inner Earth. At the time, she had played the role of damsel in distress so well that Doodles had fallen prey too easily. There had been many times that Doodles wished he could have gone back in time and not fallen for Rita's schemes. He knew it was impossible and the only thing to do was to move on and learn from it, but it still upset him when he thought about it.

"Hello, Doodles," the Emperor said. The man's voice was confident and deep.

"Hello," Doodles replied. He didn't want to say too much. It was probably better to let the Emperor do most of the talking. After all, Doodles had never met an emperor before. He wasn't quite sure how to act.

"I have heard a lot about you. You have had quite a number of adventures for someone so young and in such a short amount of time," the Emperor said. "You have the ability to draw with just your hands, an ability only the ancient Wizarts possessed. You have also demonstrated an ability to use your hands in place of dissolving ink. You are a rare specimen, Doodles Lanhorn. A rare one, indeed." Doodles didn't like the use of the word "specimen," but so far the Emperor seemed to like him.

"I meet every new Wizart. The talk I have with them for the most part is generally the same," the Emperor explained. "But not so with you, Doodles. You and I will be having a much different conversation, one that may change the face of Wizartry forever."

Doodles fidgeted nervously. He was anxious but he had to admit he was pretty excited. He wanted not only to be a Wizart, but also to help accomplish something in the Wizartry world. With the Emperor taking an interest in him, it seemed likely he could do just that. And amazingly, at the same time as helping the Wizartry world, he would also help his hometown in the real world with Detective O'Malley's cases. Life was getting interesting for a middle school student.

* * *

"You have talent and apparently great strength," the Emperor's deep voice echoed throughout the meeting chamber. His face became serious suddenly, a stark contrast to the friendly demeanor he started off with. "But your strength comes from

101

rage, a very dangerous and unreliable source of power. You will have to learn to harness this newly found power, to control your anger and learn to call up the strength only when needed. You will have to develop good, mature judgment. This will take time, practice, and patience." The Emperor smiled. "You were not summoned here for a lecture. You have compassion, resolve, creativity, a kind heart, loyalty, bravery, and a stubborn persistence to succeed. Should you ever take to a darker side, you would be the most dangerous enemy Wizartry has ever faced. We will all have to work hard and watch carefully to see that doesn't happen. But I am confident that because of all your good and honest qualities, you will make the most powerful Wizart we have ever had. I will tell you the remaining Wizartry secrets later as I do with all new Wizarts, but for now, here is where we want you to start."

The Emperor motioned to a seat next to him. "Sit down, Doodles. This is going to take a while." Doodles nodded and sat down. He was getting used to the Emperor's voice, and already had decided that the Emperor wasn't nearly as intimidating as Doodles first imagined.

The Emperor continued, "You had your original training from Riddley and that went well. I am going to place you under his tutelage again to learn to channel your power responsibly. I am sure you were surprised when you first discovered Wizartry, Doodles. Another entire world opened up to you. It is impressive that you have come so far in such a short amount of time. Although you will be the youngest competitor, I have chosen you."

Doodles sat up. "Competitor?"

"Yes," the Emperor replied. "You will represent the United States Wizarts."

"Represent for what?" Doodles asked.

The Emperor took out a piece of paper and showed it to Doodles. "I just sent this letter out to all countries. It is an invitation to the annual Wizartry Competition. Each country sends their bravest and brightest Wizarts to compete in a series of events later in the spring. The date has not been set yet so I will try to arrange for it to take place during your school's Spring Break. We would not want you to miss more school than you already have. Your education is very important."

Doodles frowned. "Shouldn't you choose someone with more experience?"

The Emperor looked at the ceiling and sighed. "Nonsense. You are my first choice. Plus, we want to develop these new powers of yours. Maybe you can teach us a thing or two."

Doodles nodded. "What about the other competitors? Do you pick them as well?"

The Emperor laughed. "No, that would make it unfair. Because I live in the United States, there are written rules that the other competitors must be picked by representatives of the other nations."

"Where is the competition held?" Doodles asked.

"Please don't worry about that right now," the Emperor replied. "You will learn all about it during your training with Riddley and your Uncle Roger. For now, I really want you to concentrate on your training and on doing well in school. Everything else will unfold at the right time.

"Our time is up now Doodles. It has been a pleasure to meet you, truly."

Doodles turned to leave and then remembered his backpack. "Wait, please, Sir. I almost forgot to return this to you. Detective O'Malley brought it to me when he came to remove my ankle monitor so I could give it back."

With that, Doodles pulled the artifact out of his bag and held it out for the Emperor to receive it. Doodles was so proud of himself for having retrieved the artifact. He was well on his way to establishing a name for himself within the Wizartry community. The Emperor turned it in his hands several times. Then he held it up before his closed eyes and stood very still for a few minutes. Doodles began to feel uneasy.

"Oh, dear," the Emperor finally said with a deep frown. "I am so sorry Doodles, but this is not our artifact. It does not emit the vibrations and aura that our ancient key was created with."

"The Mayor created a fake? I should have known! Sometimes I can be so gullible." Doodles exclaimed.

"Don't be so hard on yourself," the Emperor said. "It takes a very practiced and keen eye to tell the difference. But that means we still need you to locate the artifact."

"I'm on it," Doodles said. However, doubt crept into his mind and he wondered what he was going to do now.

* * *

Doodles took his friends Laura, Samantha and Darren to visit Detective O'Malley at the station. On the way there, Doodles spotted the bully, Ricky, walking toward them on the sidewalk. He couldn't believe how many times he ran into people that gave him trouble. Hollyport wasn't a large town but it certainly wasn't that small. Doodles figured it was his terrible luck.

"We have to stop meeting like this," Ricky said as they neared. He grabbed Doodles by the shirt collar.

"Let him go!" Laura yelled.

"I'll let him go when I'm done," Ricky said. "Just saying hi, that's all." He grabbed Doodle's shirt even tighter and brought him closer to his face. "I should throw you into the dumpster."

"I said let him go!" Laura yelled louder.

Ricky ignored her. He started to drag Doodles towards a dumpster across the street.

Samantha ran over and kicked Ricky in the shins as hard as she could. He let out a yell and let go of Doodles' shirt. Ricky knelt down and rubbed at his shin.

The group of friends took the opportunity to run off. They continued on to the police station. Ricky didn't follow.

When they arrived, they found Detective O'Malley sifting through some reports on his desk. He looked up when they entered his office.

"What's that?" O'Malley asked, gesturing to the artifact in Doodles' hands. "I thought you said you were going to return it."

Doodles placed the artifact on O'Malley's desk. "It's a phony," Doodles replied. "The real one is somewhere else."

The room became very quiet, like they were all holding their breath.

"I remember when I first came to your house, Doodles," O'Malley said. "I asked your father if you had any enemies and he said quite a few. At the time, I thought it was strange that a middle school kid would have so many people who didn't like him. Knowing who you are now, it makes more sense. I am glad you came to me for help with finding the real artifact. Where do you think Mr. Derringer might have stashed it?"

Doodles thought for a minute. "My first instinct would be to say Rita or Alanso got hold of it somehow, but they are locked away. Right?"

"I checked on them recently," O'Malley said. "They are still locked up. Looks like their lawyers are going to plead insanity. So as of now, it couldn't have been them."

"I don't know who else could have done it," Doodles admitted. "It could be with anyone or anywhere."

"No," O'Malley said. "But Hollyport isn't that big of a place. Think, Doodles. Who else might have it?"

"I don't know," Doodles said. "I just found out myself that we don't have the real one."

"Well," O'Malley said. "My gut instinct tells me that Shane Derringer is hiding something from us." O'Malley shook his head. "From what I have seen and know, it seems to me like you are always caught up in the middle of Wizartry affairs."

Doodles sighed. "I guess that's true," he admitted. "But that still doesn't change the fact that I don't know..."

Laura suddenly blurted out, "Derrick!"

"Excuse me?" O'Malley asked.

All eyes turned toward Laura. "Derrick! The limo driver! He used to work for Mayor Derringer as his personal limo driver. He's the only other person who was with us when we went after him. Remember we saw him with Mr. Derringer, Rita, and Alanso in Inner Earth? We haven't seen him since. Maybe Mr. Derringer gave it to Derrick to keep safe!"

Darren stood up. "That could be it!"

"Now, hold on a minute," O'Malley said. "Don't get too excited yet. Let me look through the files." He began to type on his computer. "Give me a second here." He started to look through a database, filling in certain information. After a few more seconds, he looked up.

"Turns out Mr. Derringer wasn't an only child. Want to know Derrick's last name? Derringer."

He turned the screen toward the kids. The Derringer profile descriptions showed that they were related. "Can you arrest him?" Laura asked.

"Sure," O'Malley said. "If we can find him. According to public records, he recently sold his house and hasn't left any paper trail since."

"Maybe we don't have to find him," Doodles said.

"What do you mean?" O'Malley asked.

Doodles said, "I have an idea."

Laura smiled. She loved it when Doodles got his ideas.

\* \* \*

Doodles looked at his friends and then back to Detective O'Malley. "I know this might not be possible, but it's an idea, and who knows, maybe it will work."

"Well, what is it?" O'Malley asked.

"We use Mr. Derringer as bait to catch his brother," Doodles said.

"That's just what I was thinking," O'Malley said. "I knew it was useful to have you on my team. I think we can offer him a plea deal to get him to help bring in his brother."

"You mean trick him?" Darren asked. "Is it okay for the police to trick people?"

"Yes, Darren. It is okay for the police to trick a suspect," O'Malley answered. "It's more of a strategy than a trick," O'Malley added.

Doodles laughed and said, "Knowing Mr. Derringer like we have come to know him, he will do anything to get ahead in life including turning in his own brother. I guess he will take a deal if offered to him. He's too selfish and greedy not to."

"Good!" O'Malley said. "I'll get the District Attorney to offer him a lesser sentence for agreeing to help us bring in his brother! Only risk being that we'll have to let him out so his brother thinks he is free and tries to reach him. We'll keep tabs on him but there is always the risk of losing both of them."

"That would be terrible," Laura said.

"We can't let him get away," Samantha said. "Laura is right. That would be awful!"

"Yes. Yes, it would be," O'Malley admitted. "But I can't have people who take part in crimes running around my town doing whatever they want. I'm glad you let me know about Mr. Derringer learning some Wizartry and about his brother knowing about it, too. I can't have criminals running around causing trouble. Not on my watch."

"So what do we do?" Doodles asked. He was ready for another adventure.

O'Malley pointed to the door of his office. "We? *We* don't do anything. You kids need to get home. Last thing I need is for your parents to call me complaining. I'll deal with the Derringer brothers. You've done a phenomenal job." And just like that, Doodles' sail that was ready to sail off on another wild adventure was deflated.

Doodles left with his friends but he felt kind of let down. His adventures with Wizartry were usually action-packed and exciting and he was able to follow them through to the end. This police stuff was strictly talk and strategizing, a boring behind-the-scenes type of brainstorming.

Maybe he could ask his parents if he could visit Inner Earth this coming weekend. He hadn't been there when there wasn't a crisis. It might be nice to take a leisurely stroll and explore it on his own time. The landscape was breathtakingly beautiful in Inner Earth. There were caves to explore and hills to climb. He could visit his old dragon friend or even visit the Wizartry retirement community. He straightened out his Wizartry hat and walked home with his friends.

* * *

Doodles was sitting in his chair, trying to finish his math homework. He hadn't heard from Detective O'Malley for a couple of days and that made concentrating on his school work harder than ever. No matter how many times he tried, he just couldn't seem to solve the problems. Maybe he should call Laura for help. She was always so good with math work. It came easy to her. It wasn't like Doodles didn't pay attention in class. He just didn't understand the formulas with all the x's and y's and a's, b's, and c's. Formulas were so confusing sometimes he couldn't even figure out what the question was, never mind the answers. Why they even had to learn them was a mystery to him.

Doodles jumped when he heard a knock on his door. He had not been expecting anyone.

"What is it?" Doodles called out, pencil still in hand.

His father's voice called back, "Doodles, Detective O'Malley is here to see you."

Doodles put the pencil down and hopped out of his chair. Maybe the detective needed him for another case. He was getting bored lately, and Doodles' parents had said he couldn't go into Inner Earth until all his school work was caught up. That felt like a long time to wait. It felt like his parents had bought him a brand new car, handed him the keys, and told him that in a few years he could take it for a drive.

He opened the door to greet the detective with a smile, but thought better of it when he saw the look on O'Malley's face.

"What? What's wrong?" Doodles asked. The detective looked like something terrible had happened.

"The Derringer brothers. Somehow they escaped," O'Malley said, confirming Doodles' suspicions.

"How? I thought you said you would be watching them!" Doodles said. He was upset. He and his friends had gone to great lengths to make sure Mr. Derringer was behind bars. He figured that once he got them all behind bars, everything would return to normal.

"We don't know how. We arrested Derrick and put him in a cell near the Mayor's so that we could listen in on their conversations. Apparently Derrick managed to smuggle in the Mayor's Wizartry supplies and he made a hole in the wall."

"I didn't think the Mayor had gotten that good at Wizartry," Doodles said. "Alanso must have taught him more than we suspected while he was in Inner Earth trying to take it over as their king."

"Well, however much training he got, it was good enough to escape," O'Malley said.

"You should never have let him out without first consulting the Wizartry Council," Uncle Roger said, entering the bedroom. "I just found out. The Council is not happy. They now have a partially trained, untrustworthy citizen with Wizartry abilities roaming around town stealing and doing whatever he wants. That is why we have rules," Uncle Roger said.

Doodles wanted to tell O'Malley that it was his fault they escaped, but realized that it was only because of his original idea that they had the opportunity to do so. Besides, playing the blame game wouldn't help locate them.

"Where could they have gone?" Doodles asked.

"By now they could be anywhere. They probably skipped town and won't come back," O'Malley said. He scratched his head irritably. "The artifact will be long gone. Let me ask you all a question. Is it possible that the Derringer brothers could teach others Wizartry?"

Uncle Roger replied, "They aren't that experienced in it, but yes, they could."

"So you're telling me they can teach a whole gang of criminals the power to create whatever they want?" O'Malley said.

He looked at Doodles. "I think we'll have to set up a meeting with your Wizartry Council. If we are going to catch these guys before they cause havoc and get back the artifact, we'll need my resources and your skills."

"Come on Doodles. I'll drive us," Uncle Roger said.

\* \* \*

Uncle Roger, Detective O'Malley, and Doodles descended the stairwell below the flower shop on Lamter Lane and into the Wizartry Council chamber. Boogley followed closely behind them. Boogley was terrified of stairs because his legs were so short. He wobbled toward the stairs and with his webbed feet he turned around backwards and slowly lowered himself, one step at a time. Doodles was used to Council Member Brian being in a foul mood, but this time all three Council members looked troubled. Doodles didn't blame them. There seemed to be problem after problem lately. He doubted they were getting much sleep.

"Detective O'Malley," Council Member Brian said. "We are not used to coordinating with non-Wizarts." Brian looked at O'Malley as if he were an intruder. Doodles hoped O'Malley wouldn't notice.

"Looks like we don't have much of a choice," O'Malley said. Doodles was happy that he didn't get upset at Brian's tone.

"What is your plan?" Council Member Holly asked.

"I'll put out a picture and a description of the Derringer brothers with a 'Be on Alert' warning for all police in the county. We'll say that one is an escapee awaiting trial and the other is a person of interest in the case.

"And once we find them," O'Malley continued, "which we will, we'll need your help. They got away last time using Wizartry. I need your people to bring them in just in case they try using Wizartry again."

Council Member Charles pointed to O'Malley and said, "We need to get this resolved as soon as possible. I say we send Roger and Doodles when you locate the Derringers. They brought him down once, they can do it again."

O'Malley shook his head. "Doodles is just a kid. I promised his father that I wouldn't put him in harm's way."

Uncle Roger spoke up, saying, "I appreciate you keeping your word but Doodles is by far the most talented Wizart we have ever seen. He's saved us more than a few times and faced trials you couldn't even imagine. He'll be fine."

Uncle Roger gave Doodles a smile.

"I agree," Holly said. "They will ride with you. Boogley, you need to stay behind. We can't have policemen seeing you. If anyone asks, they are part of your special task force."

"They would believe Roger, but they will have an issue with me taking a kid on a case," O'Malley said.

Doodles began to paint with his hands, concentrating on his face and hair. He focused on every detail, his nimble fingers working their way around his head with precision. After a few moments, O'Malley looked on in surprise as a short, middle-aged man stood in Doodles' place.

"Wizartry can be used to make disguises as well," Doodles explained to the detective.

O'Malley sighed. "I don't like it at all," he said. "But we need to get this done. Let's go."

# CHAPTER 14

Uncle Roger rode in the front passenger seat of O'Malley's squad car. Doodles took the back seat. They had been driving around the center of Hollyport for a while now. They wanted to be able to get to a sighting as fast as possible, and since they didn't know what side of town the Derringer brothers might be, it was best to stay within the middle. They listened to reports on the radio from other cruisers. Nothing had come up yet.

"What if we can't find them?" Doodles asked.

He was afraid that if he didn't come back with the real artifact, all of the progress he had made within the Wizartry world would go away. They were starting to respect him and Doodles finally felt that he had found his place in the world.

"We'll find them," O'Malley said. "I have everyone on the force looking for them."

Doodles was appreciative of O'Malley's confidence, but Doodles was mature enough to know that nothing was ever guaranteed. The long car ride gave Doodles time to think up a speech to give to the Council and the Emperor if they came back empty handed.

A woman's voice came over the police radio suddenly, saying, "Attention all units. Suspects spotted heading north on Winter Avenue toward Route Five."

Before Doodles could say something, Detective O'Malley swerved the car around, tires screeching, and sped off. Doodles was thankful he was wearing his seat belt.

"No one closes in until I get there," O'Malley said into his radio receiver. He looked over to Uncle Roger for a second and said, "Looks like the brothers are heading out of town. Get ready."

The police cruiser picked up speed and Roger took out his paint brush and held it ready. The Mayor and Derrick Derringer had not known how to use Wizartry for that long. They were outnumbered and out-skilled.

O'Malley turned the sirens on to go through a few red lights, something Doodles had always wanted to do. He remembered when he was younger playing with toy police cars, but the real thing was much neater.

As O'Malley's cruiser turned a corner and on to Winter Avenue, they spotted the fleeing white sedan.

"That's it!" O'Malley exclaimed. "Let's make it quick."

He sped up, pushing his car to its limits. The white sedan accelerated after the Derringer brothers saw the cruiser in their rearview mirror, but it was no match for O'Malley's vehicle.

They were soon right behind it.

"Pull over!" O'Malley said through his loudspeaker.

To Doodles' surprise, the car slowed down and pulled to the side.

"Get out but stay behind the car," O'Malley commanded.

O'Malley then drew his weapon and approached the car warily.

Suddenly, the Mayor and Derrick Derringer emerged from the car. They began to run. Detective O'Malley pursued immediately. Doodles and Uncle Roger looked at each other. Neither was trained for a situation like this. Uncle Roger shrugged, and then took off running, joining Detective O'Malley in the pursuit.

Shane Derringer looked back and realized he was very out of shape and the Detective would be on them soon. He grabbed his brother and threw him to the ground. "Sorry," the Mayor said as he kept running.

O'Malley had no choice but to tackle Derrick and handcuff him. Uncle Roger also was too out of shape to run much farther. He turned and called out, "Go after him, Doodles!"

There were sirens in the distance, approaching fast, but they would come too late.

"Go!" O'Malley echoed as he struggled to keep Derrick held down. "Be careful!"

As Doodles ran after Mayor Derringer, he glanced back at his uncle one more time. Uncle Roger was busy creating rope to help tie Derrick's legs together. One Derringer down, and one to go, Doodles told himself.

The Mayor was heading toward an apartment building at the end of the street. Doodles pushed himself to run faster. Doodles wasn't the best athlete, but the Mayor wasn't much of a runner. But he'd had a large lead and the apartment building was not too far away.

Doodles realized that the Mayor was going to reach the apartment building before him. Once inside the building, it might be impossible to track him. If he got away again, they might never find him. The thought made him angry.

He held out his hand as swirls of light shot outward. They extended toward the Mayor, but they whizzed by his shoulder, slamming into the building and dissipating in a cloud of paint.

With mere seconds remaining, Doodles tried again. This time the colors hit the Mayor directly in his back. The Mayor let out a scream and stumbled, falling to the ground, red and yellow paint covering his dark clothing.

Doodles ran over to him. Mr. Derringer was trying to get up but the force of the shooting paint had knocked the wind out of him. Doodles quickly drew handcuffs and put them on Mr. Derringer's wrists. He began to search him, frantically looking for the artifact.

"Where is it?" Doodles yelled.

The Mayor finally caught his breath and sat up wheezing as he sucked in a big gulp of air. Paint ran down his back and shoulders. "I... will never tell you," he said to Doodles.

The sirens in the background were very close now. Soon the rest of the police would be on them and Doodles wouldn't be able to ask all the questions he needed to or explain who he was.

"Tell me!" Doodles pleaded.

"Help me out and I'll tell you exactly where it is," Mr. Derringer said.

Doodles didn't like the sudden turn in Mr. Derringer's willingness to hand over the artifact. Doodles didn't trust the man at all, but at this point, Doodles was desperate. The Emperor was counting on him to get the artifact back. Doodles knew Laura and Darren would be mad at him for letting Mr. Derringer go, but this seemed like the only option.

"If you help me escape, I promise I'll leave town and never return. I'll also tell you where the artifact is," Mr. Derringer said. He sounded so sincere, so desperate, that Doodles found himself starting to believe him.

Doodles didn't have time for games. "Fine, tell me where it is. I'll help you. And you better not show your face around here ever again! You better hurry. Once they get here, I can't stop them from arresting you."

Mr. Derringer sighed. "I had Derrick put it in a safe deposit box at Hollyport Union Bank. Box number three-hundred thirty-three. Now get me out of here."

Mr. Derringer struggled to stand up and Doodles assisted him. Doodles spotted a manhole cover and slid it aside. Then he removed the handcuffs. He pointed. "Off you go before I change my mind," Doodles said.

"Down there?" Mr. Derringer asked. "But it's disgusting..."

Doodles shrugged. "Not my problem, and if you lied about the artifact, I will find you."

Mr. Derringer heard shouts approaching their location. He took in a deep breath and jumped down. Doodles didn't wait to see if he was okay. He closed the manhole cover and stood there waiting for the police to get closer. He felt sick. Explaining to Detective O'Malley why he had let Mr. Derringer go was going to be awful.

* * *

"You did what?" Detective O'Malley yelled. "How could you do that?"

Doodles shrugged. "I had no choice. We wanted to know where the artifact was, right?"

O'Malley took a deep breath and let the air out slowly. "I'm really trying to be patient, here. We were supposed to work *together*. We need to follow protocol. We could have just brought him in and questioned him."

Doodles replied, "We would never be able to question him about the artifact because we couldn't bring up Wizartry in front of anyone else."

O'Malley said, "You realize you could be arrested for aiding a criminal in escaping? This is bad. You showed poor judgment, Doodles. Now the artifact is still missing and Mr. Derringer is gone. We are in a much worse position than when we started."

Doodles shifted nervously. O'Malley looked really upset.

"I did what I thought was right. We needed the artifact. We have the safe deposit box number at the bank," Doodles said. "We can go there and retrieve the artifact now."

"Doodles. The man is a liar. What makes you think it's actually in there or that he gave you the right numbers?" O'Malley asked.

Doodles realized that O'Malley might very well be right. Mr. Derringer had never told him the truth, so why would this time be any different? Doodles tried to explain, "Because he looked so sincere. I could see it in his eyes that he was really scared and just wanted to get away," Doodles said but as he said it and as the adrenaline of the chase was now wearing off, he realized the Mayor might have fooled him again.

"I'll have to get a warrant to open and search the safe deposit box," O'Malley said. "Those are not easy to come by. If the artifact is not in there, we are back to step one. Except this time, Shane Derringer will be long gone." O'Malley combed back his hair with his hand and sighed.

"It's in there," Doodles said.

"Let's hope you're right, kid," O'Malley said.

* * *

Doodles thankfully changed back into his regular, thirteen-year-old form. It wasn't easy pretending to be someone he was not. While he waited for Detective O'Malley to obtain a search warrant for the safe deposit box, he decided to stop by Riddley's store on Lamter Lane. It was there that Doodles always found a way to refocus. Riddley was eccentric, but he did give good advice.

Riddley was happy to see him and was encouraging, despite the news Doodles gave him of Mr. Derringer's escape.

"Congratulations on becoming a Wizart," Riddley said sincerely. "I knew you could do it. After all, I'm the one who trained you."

Doodles laughed. "So you knew about the Emperor this whole time?"

"Of course," Riddley replied. "And he reached out to me recently, telling me that I am to train you for the annual International Wizartry Competition."

Riddley had been filling small jars of paint from larger containers, but now that they were in conversation, Riddley put the container down and wiped some of the excess paint off of his hand with a clean rag.

"What is the competition?" Doodles asked.

Riddley said, "It is held once a year. The best of the best Wizarts, representing every country in the world, are sent to compete at whichever country is hosting. It is a week-long event. You'll meet Wizarts from all over the world, learn things you've never imagined, and represent your country with pride. I might even place a bet on you. It's my favorite part, the betting. There will be a variety of vendors of Wizartry products with trinkets, antiques, and dyes and paints of all different colors from exotic locations. There will be performances and networking and plenty to do!"

Doodles smiled. "It sounds fun!" With all of the problems and adventures he had been through lately, it would be nice to have some relaxing fun for a change.

Riddley laughed. "Oh, it is. But even though there are plenty of people to meet, shows to see, and things to discover, you will also find yourself under a lot of pressure. The United States has not won an International Wizartry Competition in over ten years. It is time to bring that title back."

"I'll do my best," Doodles said, realizing his dream of being able to relax and enjoy was short lived.

"Good, because some of the competitors this year are among the most talented Wizarts I have ever seen," Riddley said. "I don't want to scare you. I only want you to take our training seriously. This is going to test your limits, Doodles."

Doodles nodded.

"Good. Let's begin," Riddley said. "And don't knock over any of my paint. I spent all morning organizing it."

\* \* \*

Doodles came home exhausted. Riddley had really pushed him today. His arms felt like lead weights. His brain felt fried from thinking so hard. Doodles had thought math class was hard. Math class was nothing compared to what he had been expected to accomplish today.

He slumped onto the living room couch. His father looked up from his newspaper. "How's everything going?" he asked.

Doodles sighed. "I'm tired."

Mr. Lanhorn laughed. "You look like it. Why don't you try and get some rest? Wouldn't hurt you to go to bed early for a change."

Doodles sat up with a groan. "I'm too tired to argue about staying up," he said.

He began to walk up the stairs, when the phone rang.

He stopped halfway up the stairs as his father called out," Doodles, wait! The phone's for you."

Doodles rolled his eyes. Even that effort hurt his head. He figured he was already half way up the stairs; his mind was set on sinking into his blankets and pillow.

"Who is it?" Doodles called down the stairs. If it was one of his friends, they would have to wait until tomorrow. He was too tired to have a long conversation.

"It's Detective O'Malley. He says it's urgent," his father responded.

Doodles put his exhaustion aside and hustled back down the stairs. "Hello?" he said when his father handed him the phone. Maybe the detective had some good news about the artifact case.

"Doodles," O'Malley said from the other end. "Bad news. There was nothing in the safe deposit box except a piece of paper with the numbers twenty-one, thirty-two, and nineteen. Whatever that means, it is probably a hint to remind him of where to find it. What is strange is that no one had used that box in over two months according to the bank's records. The Mayor must have planned this a long time ago. But he is gone now and all we have is this one clue. We still have his brother at least, but the Mayor won't come back for him. We already saw that when he tripped him to get away."

"What can we do?" Doodles asked. Doodles was starting to get used to being frustrated. He clenched his fist and tried to take a few deep breaths to calm himself down.

"Honestly?" O'Malley asked. "Cut our losses and move on. Wherever the artifact is, it is long gone."

"We can't just give up!" Doodles yelled. He felt calmer when he sensed his father's reassuring hand on his shoulder. Doodles realized that he couldn't explain the significance of the Wizartry artifact to the detective but he needed him to understand how important the artifact was to the safety of all Wizarts. He gave a concerned look to his father before speaking into the phone again.

"Can't we do something?"

"Trust me. I don't like leaving cases unsolved. But this case has gone cold. We have no leads left. These numbers mean nothing to us," O'Malley said.

"We have to get the artifact back," Doodles pleaded. "We just have to!"

"I appreciate your enthusiasm," O'Malley said. "But like I said, it would be like finding a needle in a haystack at this point. This isn't my only case, you know."

"Give me time to think of something," Doodles said. "I just know it's here."

"I'll be here if you think of something," O'Malley said. "But until then, I can't be driving around aimlessly. It's a waste of my time and the taxpayers' money." Then he hung up the phone.

Doodles looked at his father.

Mr. Lanhorn patted him on the back. "It will work out," he said.

Doodles wasn't so sure, but he had to think, and he did his best thinking when he was with his friends. Forgetting about his exhaustion, he said, "Dad, can I call Laura and Samantha and Darren to come over tonight?"

His father nodded.

"We have work to do," Doodles said and headed upstairs.

Boogley greeted him as soon as he entered the room. Boogley had one of Doodles' shoes in his mouth and was gnawing on it. He let it drop to the floor when he saw Doodles' expression. "What's wrong? Did the detective find the artifact?"

Doodles shook his head. "No, but with your help and my friends, we need to figure it out."

# Chapter 15

Laura, Samantha, Darren, Doodles, and Boogley sat on the floor of Doodles' bedroom. They had tossed a few ideas around, but nothing seemed like a viable plan.

"I don't know, Doodles," Darren said. "I just can't think of anything useful." Doodles noted that Darren looked unusually discouraged.

Laura sighed. "Me neither," she said. "We want to help, but maybe Detective O'Malley is right. Maybe the artifact is long gone. I'm so sorry, Doodles." Doodles didn't like seeing his friends upset. He felt bad enough that he brought them into this situation.

Boogley hopped up and down in frustration. "If that Mayor were here I would sink my teeth right into his toes. That would show him!"

Doodles patted Boogley's head. "Calm down," he said. "There has to be a way." Doodles strained his brain for something, anything that would help them locate Mr. Derringer. His first thought was that the man might still be covered in paint from when he used his powers. But that thought was quickly dismissed because he would be long gone and the water down in the sewers would make it impossible to track using that method.

Then a thought occurred to Doodles and he was surprised that none of them had thought of it beforehand. All of them had been so focused on finding Mr. Derringer that they forgot about the numbers on the piece of paper.

"I got it!" Doodles exclaimed. "The numbers on the paper, they must be for a lock combination." He jumped up in excitement, startling Boogley.

Darren perked up. "A locker combination? Maybe at the school? What were the numbers on the piece of paper?"

Doodles tried to remember what O'Malley had told him over the phone. "I think they were twenty-two, thirty-two, and nineteen," he said.

Laura asked, "Doodles, are you sure?"

Doodles nodded. "I'm pretty sure, yeah. Why?"

Darren stood up and said, "Doodles, I remember seeing a file cabinet in Mr. Derringer's office when I was looking through the drawers the day we snuck in there. There was a lock on it. I'm almost positive. It's got to be in there."

Samantha nodded. "I remember there being a lock on the file cabinet too," she said.

"Let's go!" Doodles said.

\* \* \*

The next day, Detective O'Malley picked up Doodles, Laura, Samantha, and Darren. They had called him last night to let him know their new idea. He got a warrant quickly issued from a judge to search on school grounds.

"The judge is going to start thinking this is one big, wild goose chase," O'Malley said. "I need to bring this case to a close soon. They don't just hand out search warrants like candy."

"It's going to be in his office," Doodles said. "He probably stashed it in there thinking he was going to pick it up the next day. But he never got a chance to."

"Don't get your hopes up," O'Malley said as he drove to the school. "If it was in the locker, he could have just told you to search there instead of sending us to the safe deposit box."

"Maybe he wanted us to be distracted for longer so it takes the heat off of us searching for him," Laura suggested.

"Maybe," O'Malley said. "You never know with that guy."

O'Malley pulled right up to the front curb of the school. They hopped out and proceeded into the school. The lone security guard let them inside with a grin when O'Malley showed him the warrant.

The security guard pointed down the hallway to the right. "His office is down there," he said, even though the kids already knew the way.

They followed the security guard down the hallway and to the Principal's office. The door Boogley had chewed up had been replaced with a stronger, metal door. The security guard opened it with his keys and then waved them inside. "I'll be down the hall if you need anything else," he said. O'Malley and the rest of them waited until the security guard was down the hall and out of sight and earshot.

"I think I remember the locker was behind this cabinet door," Darren told them.

"Let's see if that combination opens it," O'Malley said. He grabbed the lock and turned the combination. It went click and snapped open. O'Malley didn't hesitate. He opened the locker and sighed.

"Another piece of paper," O'Malley said. He turned to Doodles. "Listen. It's clear that he is messing with us. Your friend Laura is right. Classic misdirection to keep our minds off of finding him.

This is a waste of our time. I'm calling this search off," O'Malley said.

"At least read the paper," Doodles pleaded. "Maybe he was just being careful."

O'Malley sighed before looking at the writing on the piece of paper. "Look," he said. "Even if this says to look somewhere else, this is a wild goose chase. You know that, right?"

Doodles shrugged. "I just don't get it. He seemed so sincere."

O'Malley said, "Good liars believe what they are saying. It's what makes them such great liars because they think they aren't lying." He looked at the paper and read, "If you are reading this, I am far away. The artifact is mine."

O'Malley crumbled the paper up into a ball and threw it on the ground. "My entire career I have brought criminals down. This guy is making me look like an amateur," he said.

"He tricked me," Doodles said. "This is all my fault."

Samantha patted his arm reassuringly and Doodles blushed.

"Nonsense," O'Malley said. "We were all tricked. I'll put out a description of Mr. Derringer to nearby towns but it doesn't look good. This guy had everything planned out well beforehand. He even concocted this wild goose chase in case he was caught." O'Malley looked around the office for anything else that might help but gave up when he didn't see anything promising.

"What can we do?" Laura asked. Doodles could have sworn Laura gave Samantha a jealous look but maybe he was imagining it.

"Nothing," O'Malley said and shrugged. "Come on. I'll drive you kids home."

"Wait," Doodles said. "What about Derrick?"

"What about him?" O'Malley asked. O'Malley was starting to look irritated and Doodles didn't want him to become upset at him.

"Maybe he knows something," Doodles suggested. "Maybe he will tell us since his own brother knocked him down to save himself."

"Why is this artifact so important to get back?" O'Malley asked. He gave Doodles a curious look.

Doodles wasn't expecting that question. "It just is. It's valuable to Wizarts."

"I don't like you keeping secrets from me," O'Malley said. "Especially if we are going to be working together. I know when you are holding something back. I'm a good read of people." He rubbed his eyes. "Look, I'm tired," O'Malley said. "I'll take you home and then I'll have a chat with Derrick Derringer. I'll try my best, but if it doesn't lead to anything, I can't waste my time on this case anymore."

"Thank you," Doodles said. "That's all I'm asking for."

\* \* \*

Detective O'Malley took a deep breath before walking into the interrogation room. Mayor Derringer's brother, Derrick, hadn't done much since he had been charged with resisting arrest. He had refused to speak to anyone. Why the man was protecting a brother who had so willingly given him up to the police was beyond O'Malley. Most likely, Derrick would only be imprisoned for a year at most. But he didn't have to let Derrick know that. O'Malley had learned that sometimes bending the truth or not revealing all the facts was a good way to get someone to talk.

He walked in with a stern look on his face. The man looked pathetic, sitting at the table with his head slumped over in defeat. O'Malley almost felt pity for the man, but he had to play the tough guy. Derrick looked up from the table with a sad look on his face. O'Malley sat down and pretended to sift through papers in his folder. He wanted to let Derrick be nervous for a little longer. It felt like a cruel tactic but he needed Derrick to give in and share what he knew.

After a few minutes he finally looked at Derrick and said, "You're in big trouble."

"I'm sorry," Derrick said, a pleading look on his face. "Please. I was just trying to help my brother."

"Your brother?" O'Malley asked. "You mean the same brother that made you his hired help when he was mayor? The same brother who knocked you down so he could get away?"

"It's not like that," Derrick said. "I had trouble finding a job. He was nice enough to give me a chance. He might be tough, but he loves me and he's family." Derrick was sweating despite the cool air conditioning.

"After all he's done to you, you're still defending him," O'Malley said. He laughed. "He'll be a free man and you will be behind bars for a long, long time."

"I can't go to jail," Derrick said, his voice quivering in fear. "Please."

"You have two options," O'Malley said. He held up two fingers for emphasis. "One, you can go to jail and best of luck to you in there; or two, you can tell me where Shane and the artifact are and I'll do my best to make sure you don't go to jail."

O'Malley could see that Derrick was conflicted, but he was still on the fence. He just needed another push in the right direction. Swaying a person was a science and O'Malley had gotten good at it over the years.

"I'm not sure you would make it in jail for long," O'Malley said, and shook his head in sympathy. "It's really a shame, being locked up in a cell for so long with nothing to do. Unfortunately, your fellow prisoners are not big fans of the former mayor. They might not like you."

"Okay!" Derrick blurted out, his eyes filling up with tears. "I'll talk! Just please don't send me to jail!"

"Good," Detective O'Malley said. "So talk."

Derrick tried to compose himself but he looked like a mess. He rubbed at his runny nose with his sleeve. "He had me to take the artifact to a small town called Pentacoast. He said we were going to go there and lay low until he could figure out how to use the artifact. That's all I know!"

O'Malley smiled. "See, that wasn't that hard. Now pull yourself together and sit tight. I can't get you out until we get your brother and the artifact back. And I hope for your sake that, unlike your brother, you are telling the truth."

* * *

Doodles waited outside of his house on the front steps. Detective O'Malley had called him about ten minutes ago and said he was on his way over. He didn't say what for. Hopefully it wasn't more bad news. Doodles wasn't sure if he could handle more bad news at this point.

It felt more like thirty minutes passed before Doodles recognized Detective O'Malley's police cruiser coming down the street. He stood up in anticipation. O'Malley parked in front of his house and got out. He was holding a bag. Doodles' heart skipped a beat. He tried to get a read on O'Malley's face to determine if he brought good or bad news, but his face was blank.

When he was about two feet away, O'Malley put the bag on the ground. He was about to say something to Doodles when O'Malley's phone rang.

"Hello?" O'Malley said after pulling his cell phone out of his pants pocket. Doodles waited impatiently as the detective talked to one of his coworkers about a boring question on how to fill out paperwork properly. The suspense was killing him.

Finally, O'Malley put the phone back into his pocket and smiled at Doodles. "Here you go, kid," O'Malley said and picked up the bag and handed it to Doodles. Doodles peered inside and saw the artifact. The emeralds around the top glowed so brightly. It felt surprisingly lighter than he thought it would.

"Yes!" Doodles cheered.

His neighbor, Mrs. Porter, looked at him from the next yard and Doodles gave an awkward wave in return. O'Malley gave him a look as if to say, "Calm down."

"We've got Shane Derringer in jail. The museum has agreed to put the fake artifact on display," the detective continued. "They said they'll call it a 'replica'.

"Now, make sure to take this genuine artifact back to its rightful owners right away," O'Malley said. "Don't want it to get lost again. Not after all that work." He turned to leave and then looked back over his shoulder. "Oh, and nice detective work, junior detective. I'll be calling on you again soon for help."

He waved goodbye, got in the car and drove off.

Doodles was so excited that he nearly tripped over the steps and dropped the artifact. He caught himself and then proceeded to the inside of his house. Imagine if after all of that he broke the artifact.

Uncle Roger was visiting, watching television in the living room. He was happy to drive Doodles to the flower shop to visit the Wizartry Council and the Emperor. They would be pleased to learn that Rita, Alanso, Loric, and Mr. Derringer were all now behind bars and that the real artifact was returned to its rightful owners.

"I'm proud of you, Doodles. You never gave up, not even when you were feeling very discouraged," Uncle Roger said as he drove.

"Thanks," Doodles replied.

"I'm serious. You saved Inner Earth from a major security issue. With the artifact back in our hands, we can ensure Inner Earth's safety."

Doodles nodded and said, "I'm just glad it worked out."

"Now that all of this is behind you," Uncle Roger continued, "I want you to really concentrate on your training with Riddley. The Competition isn't that far off."

"I will," Doodles replied. If only the kids at school knew Doodles was representing the entire United States in a competition. They always picked him last for any sport and constantly made fun of him for his lack of hand-eye coordination. Unfortunately, they would never know he had special talents. Such was the life of a Wizart.

"We just got confirmation that the competition will be held here, in Hollyport," Uncle Roger said as they neared the flower shop on Lamter Lane. "Over the next few months, Wizarts from all over the world will be flying to our small town. You'll get to meet them and learn from them. It is an exciting time!"

Doodles felt excited but also apprehensive. He knew he had talent, but he was young, and these Wizarts from around the world were far more experienced.

Doodles was so lost in his thoughts that he didn't realize that his uncle had already parked in front of the flower shop.

"The Emperor and Council will want to speak to you on your own," Uncle Roger said. "See you tonight for dinner!" He waved and drove off, leaving Doodles by himself with the artifact.

\* \* \*

"Let me see it," the Emperor said, holding out his hands.

Doodles took the artifact and gave it to the Emperor. For a few seconds, Doodles worried he had brought another fake artifact.

The Emperor turned it around a few times, looking it over very carefully, and then smiled. "This is it," the Emperor said. "Good work!"

The Emperor placed the artifact on the table and looked at Doodles. "Doodles Lanhorn," the Emperor said. "Bringing the artifact back reinforces my selection of you as the representative of the United States in the upcoming International Wizartry Competition. We have some exciting news for you. I'll let Council Member Charles tell you."

Charles grinned and put his pen down. "Hello, Doodles. You are among the first few to know that as of tomorrow, I will be officially retiring to Inner Earth. Already painted my house there." He looked around and said, "I will miss this place and its duties, but my body can't handle the stress it requires."

"I'm sorry to hear that you're leaving us," Doodles said, unsure how to respond. He really would miss Charles.

"It is past my time," Charles said. "I probably should have retired years ago, but so much happened so fast that it didn't seem right to leave yet. Now that things have calmed down for the time being, it makes more sense. But, that will leave the Wizartry Council one seat short. There always needs to be three members. Therefore, the winner of this year's Competition will take his or her place on the Wizartry Council bypassing the election process."

Doodles couldn't believe what he had just heard. "Aren't I too young for the Council?" he asked. Doodles remembered back to his Wizartry test in front of the Council in which they had contested his young age.

The Emperor laughed. "Always the worrier," he said. "You seem to be pretty confident that you will be the winner, but you haven't won it yet, Doodles. According to our ancient laws, there is no age requirement to sit on the Council, as long as you are a full Wizart. However, I need you to know I want you to win this competition. I want your skills and creative mind on my Council. That is why I fought so hard to have the Competition here and for you to represent the United States."

"I'm... I'm flattered," Doodles said. He tried to keep a straight face, but he knew he must have been smiling like he did when opening a gift on Christmas morning.

"I am pretty sure you will win the Competition, you will earn your seat on the Wizartry Council by my side, and you will help shape the future of all Wizarts," the Emperor declared.

# CHAPTER 16

Riddley looked at the clock on the wall as the second hand neared the twelve. "And... go!" He yelled out.

Doodles began to paint with his hands, moving them about with swirls of color. He had to move about the room to paint what was required. His arms were growing sore. He had to stretch them out for a few seconds and then continued.

"Time!" Riddley yelled. Doodles put his hands down reluctantly. A few seconds later there was a popping sound and a wall of bricks appeared.

Riddley shook his head in disappointment. He walked up to the wall and pointed to an entire missing corner. "Why didn't you finish it?" Riddley asked.

Doodles rubbed at his shoulder. "My arms are sore. There wasn't enough time," Doodles said.

Riddley replied, "There is enough time. Your arms just aren't strong enough to keep up. Remember, this is a week-long competition and most of the candidates are significantly older, and physically stronger than you."

Doodles sat down in a chair, sweat running down his face. "I'm trying," he said.

"I know," Riddley emphasized. "But I promised the Emperor you would have a good shot at winning. Creativity, heart, effort, and skill are not where you are lacking. In fact, you are probably one of the best in all of those categories. Where you are lacking, and what will give the other competitors a major advantage over you, are your speed and your endurance."

"So, what am I supposed to do?" Doodles asked. "I've never lifted weights at the gym before and I don't run much."

"Catch your breath and then carry this home," Riddley said. Doodles looked around. "Carry what home?"

Riddley took out his paint brush and created a bucket full of heavy rocks. "Carry this bucket home and then return it to me tomorrow morning."

Doodles gave Riddley a quizzical look and when he realized Riddley wasn't joking, Doodles stood up and lifted the bucket. His arms strained and he could barely walk. "It's going to take me forever to get home with this," Doodles complained. "It's got to be close to fifty pounds!"

Riddley smiled. "So you better start now. Oh, and Doodles, one more thing. No cheating and using Wizartry to create a wheelbarrow or anything of the sort. This is part of the training."

Doodles didn't want to waste his energy arguing. He set off with the bucket, his knees wobbly and his face set in determination.

It took Doodles almost three hours to get home. He had to stop many times along the way. He even had to stop at a store and buy a bottle of water with his allowance money. Doodles almost drank the entire bottle in one gulp. When he finally got home, he dropped the bucket onto the bottom stairs of his front porch and let out a gigantic sigh of relief. His arms and legs were on fire, a persistent pain and soreness. He didn't care that he was all sweaty and still wearing his clothes. He barely made it up the stairs, plopped onto his bed with shoes still on, and fell into a deep sleep.

* * *

This continued for several weeks. Each day, Doodles would attend school, aching and completely exhausted, go to Riddley's shop for more training, and then carry home a bucket of rocks. Each morning before school, Doodles dropped off the bucket. He was beginning to resent the very sight of rocks.

Yesterday was no exception. Luckily, this morning was the start of Winter Break and Doodles didn't have to go to school for almost two weeks. So far this had been a mild winter and Hollyport had not had its first snowfall. He lay in bed, awake, yet unwilling to get out of bed. He didn't weigh much, but in that moment he felt like he weighed a ton.

His cell phone rang. It was Samantha.

"Hello," Doodles answered.

"Doodles, I was wondering if you wanted to catch a movie this week with me," Samantha said on the other end of the line.

Doodles swallowed. "With me, or the group?"

"Just you, silly," Samantha said.

Doodles' heart leapt out of his chest. He really liked her. She was beautiful, smart, funny, and she was way out of his league.

"Uh, sure. I mean yes," he replied.

They talked a bit more and then Doodles lay there several minutes after the conversation ended. He couldn't believe his luck. Maybe she just thought of him as a friend, but either way he was excited to spend more time with her.

His Dad had asked him a few times already if he wanted to have breakfast. It wasn't Pancake Saturday, so there was no real motivation to get up. Besides, he had a lot of daydreaming to do. Finally, he rolled over and sat up. The light came streaming in through the window. Surprisingly, his muscles felt stiff but not in a painful way like he had felt the last few weeks. He stretched and got out of bed. He walked downstairs to join his family in the kitchen. They were already done eating and had cleared the plates.

"Eat up," his mother said as she fetched a new plate of eggs and bacon and placed it in front of him. "They're a little cold but should still be good." She smiled at him.

Doodles finished his breakfast and hurried outside. He bent down and picked up the bucket. To his surprise, it didn't feel as heavy as it had before. Maybe all this carrying it back and forth was actually making him stronger. When he wasn't holding the bucket of rocks, his arms and legs felt so light and free.

He made it to Riddley's shop in what must have been a personal record, only stopping twice to catch his breath.

"I'll give you a few minutes to rest," Riddley said when Doodles entered the shop.

"I'm ready," Doodles said.

Riddley turned around in surprise and smiled. "Don't need to catch your breath? Impressive."

Doodles took his place in the center of the room.

"There is going to be one test a day at the Competition," Riddley explained. "Each test will be completely different and address a variety of skill sets. The winning nation of each day gets one point. The final day winner gets two points. There have been a few Competitions in which the final day gave the second place nation a boost to first place." Riddley grinned. "At the end of each day," he said, "there are celebrations, shows, and a chance to share news. That is when you will feel you really want to join in the celebration, eat the exotic food and be mesmerized by the shows. These are just distractions. You will want to keep your eyes and ears open, Doodles. The good Wizarts don't get caught up in the celebrations; instead, they learn their opponents' weaknesses and strengths, and fears. They then use this knowledge on the playing field."

Doodles nodded. "I will pay attention."

Riddley raised one eyebrow. "You say that now, but you are still a kid, Doodles. It will take all of your effort to remain distraction-free with so much going on. A lot of Wizarts from all over the world have heard of your exploits so far and will want to talk to you. Let them. It is unavoidable, but don't lose focus. Wizarts from all over the world will come to watch the competition. A lot of nations will be vying to win. Who doesn't want a representative on the Council?"

Riddley looked at the clock on the wall. "You have five minutes to make a cage you think will hold a beast I am going to create. Good luck!"

Riddley began to paint. Doodles started as well. He tried not to worry about what it was that Riddley was creating. That would only waste time. He needed to focus on what material would be the strongest for his cage. Undoubtedly, it would be a powerful creature and the bars of the cage would have to hold it in.

"Four minutes left!" Riddley called out.

Doodles decided on steel bars on the cage. He stepped back as Riddley finished and he too stepped back.

He made sure the cage bars covered all around the area Riddley had painted. He didn't have time to watch what Riddley was painting or try to guess what it was.

Riddley laughed when the cage appeared. Doodles wondered why he laughed, but then moaned as a giant garden snake appeared inside of the cage. It was very long, but it was also very skinny.

It looked around the cage, its forked tongue sticking out. It moved toward the cell bars and slithered between them. When it was halfway out, Riddley took a bottle of dissolving ink from a pouch at his side and poured it over the snake.

"And that is why you focus on everything, not just the task at hand," Riddley said. "If you had, you would have noticed I was drawing a snake. The bars on your cage are strong enough to hold a gorilla, but they are placed too far apart. Try to cover as many options as you can. A sturdy cage with bars close together would hold both a giant gorilla and a snake."

Doodles shook his head. "I was so focused on how to make a strong cage, I didn't even think about anything else."

Riddley nodded. "I know. And there was a good chance your cage would hold if I decided to create something large. But I didn't, and you just lost. Each and every point in the Competition matters. Your competitors would be one point ahead of you. You need to look at the larger picture. Don't just narrow your sight on one direction. Five minutes is a long time if you utilize your time appropriately."

Doodles sighed. "I have a lot to learn," he said.

Riddley said, "You do. But Wizartry is never truly mastered. Everyone learns over the course of their entire life. Unfortunately, we are almost out of time to train. But you are stronger physically and mentally. You have a good shot at winning the International Wizartry Competition if you really put your mind to it, Doodles. If you make the seat on the Council, you will have the power to change Wizartry forever."

Doodles hoped Riddley was right.

# CHAPTER 17

"I am sure you were surprised when you first discovered Wizartry, Doodles," the Wizartry Emperor said in a deep voice. "Another entire world opened up to you. Well, I have another secret to tell you, one that only the Wizartry Council, myself, and a few others we call the Wizartry Guardians know about. This secret will take precedence before the International Wizartry Competition begins. We introduced you to Inner Earth, and you have earned free access. However, although Wizarts across the world know that we guard the entrance between Hollyport and Inner Earth, not many know that the Wizartry Guardians also guard another entrance."

Doodles sat up. "There is another entrance? I was told there was only one."

"Yes," the Emperor replied. "But not another entrance from the outer world to Inner Earth.

"There is a whole other world, Doodles. It is a dark and scary place. We call it Center Earth because it is closer to the Earth's mantle, even deeper than Inner Earth. There are dark and evil beings there. It is in constant darkness. The absence of light is the absence of color, and the beings there despise color. The gates were sealed a long, long time ago and the Wizartry Guardians are tasked with making sure that gate stays forever sealed."

"Why are you telling me this now, right before the Competition?" Doodles asked.

The Emperor took out a piece of paper. "I just received this letter. It is from the Wizartry Guardians. Somehow, after centuries, the seal is breaking. It will only be a matter of time until Inner Earth is open to that hideous Center Earth. This is terrible timing with the Competition almost upon us."

Doodles frowned. "What are we going to do? What lives there in Center Earth?"

The Emperor looked at the ceiling and sighed. He looked to Doodles as though he were remembering a time in his past. "There are creatures in there, some human-like, others completely alien. Each one is able to destroy things that were created by Wizartry. The very ground they walk on becomes corrupted and is ripped of every nutrient and color. They are cruel and intent on only one thing: destroying anything to do with Wizartry."

Doodles realized that even though Inner Earth was a truly beautiful, unique and magical land, it was constantly beset by enemies. Doodles agreed with the Emperor that this was far more important than any competition at the moment. "What can we do to stop Center Earth from invading Inner Earth?" Doodles asked. "Can't we just ask all the Wizards from other countries to assist since everyone is flying here for the Competition?

"No. The number of Wizarts that need to know about the entrance to Center Earth must be kept to a minimum in order to maintain control. That's where you come in to play," the Emperor said. "The Wizartry Guardians are hand-picked by me. They are the best of the best Wizarts from all over the world. There are ten of them currently and they are all sworn to secrecy about the entrance. They take shifts in two groups of five. But even though they are the most skilled Wizarts, none of them possess your capabilities, Doodles. None of them possess the amount of creativity you have. I can trust you with this secret, Doodles. I task you, Doodles Lanhorn, on behalf of the Emperor, on behalf of Inner Earth and Wizarts all over the world, with coming up with a creative solution to this problem."

Doodles gulped. "How long do we have?" He asked.

"Days, maybe a week," the Emperor responded. "It's too hard to tell. We will have you go and meet with all of the members of the Wizartry Guardians. Once you see the gate to Center Earth and speak with them, I am confident you will come up with a solution. I will put a hold on the Competition until then. I want your mind fully focused on fixing the gate. The competition can wait."

"I will do my best," Doodles said and he meant it.

"We don't need your best. We need this resolved immediately," the Emperor said.

Doodles nodded. If he wanted to be on the Wizartry Council, he would have to prove his worth to the Emperor and Wizartry Council by winning the tournament and keeping the gate to Center Earth sealed. Doodles gulped audibly. The road ahead would not be easy.

The End

# ABOUT THE AUTHOR

Russell D. Bernstein was born and raised in Miami, Florida; he currently resides in Orange, Connecticut with his family. He has a Masters in Organizational Leadership and extensive experience in the healthcare field. The author used that knowledge as background for his writing and his talks at schools. For more on Russell D. Bernstein, go to his website: http://www.bullytalks.com.

Other novels by Russell D. Bernstein
Published by Hannacroix Creek Books, Inc.

*Doodles Lanhorn and the Quest to Save Inner Earth*

Russell D. Bernstein

2016   134 pages

Doodles Lanhorn is a red-headed boy of thirteen who doesn't feel very popular or successful but he does have a special talent: he has recently discovered the powers of Wizartry, the art of drawing something and making it come to life. Doodles comes to learn that he is unique in that he does not require a paint brush like most Wizarts; he can draw with just the use of his hands. In *Doodles Lanhorn and the Quest to Save Inner Earth*, Doodles must deal with old enemies, rescue his family, and ultimately save Inner Earth, the sacred land of the Wizarts. With the help of his friends Laura, Darren, and Boogley, a very unique and special creature, Doodles is able to overcome his fears so he can face all these obstacles, head on.

"A modern day fable of an innovative boy using his creativity to develop strategies to successfully defeat bullying."
—Paula Fradiani, Ed.D., child advocate

"*Doodles Lanhorn and the Quest to Save Inner Earth* is a great read. Bernstein did an excellent job in pacing the plot, and the detail was extraordinary. Doodles. The main character, was especially enjoyable—smart and loyal to a fault. I would recommend this book to all of my peers and classmates and hope that they love it as much as I did."
—C.J., 12-year-old seventh grader

www.ingramcontent.com/pod-product-compliance
Lightning Source LLC
Chambersburg PA
CBHW020624250626
47154CB00004B/1647